BRENDEL'S FANTASY

BRENDEL'S FANTASY

GÜNTHER FREITAG

Translated from the German by
Eugene H. Hayworth

First published in Germany under the title *Brendels Fantasie* by Günther Freitag
Copyright © 2009 by Edition Elke Heidenreich
A division of Verlagsgruppe Random House, München Germany
Translation copyright © 2012 Eugene H. Hayworth

First published in Great Britain in 2012 by
HAUS PUBLISHING LTD.
70 Cadogan Place, London SW1X 9AH
www.hauspublishing.com

ISBN 978 1 907822 53 7
ebook ISBN 978 1 907822 54 4

Typeset in Garamond by MacGuru Ltd
info@macguru.org.uk

Printed in Great Britain by CPI Group (UK) Ltd, Croydon, CR0 4YY

A CIP catalogue for this book is available from the British Library

Death seemed like a puppeteer to him,
who quickly needs a Duke.

Rainer Maria Rilke

ALTHOUGH HIS FAVORITE SONATA on the programme is scheduled for after the intermission, Höller leaves the Palazzo Papesse and takes the narrow street down the hill to the Piazza del Campo. There are only a few people on the road with him on this cold, damp autumn evening, most of them sporting turned-up collars with scarves draped artfully around their necks, as the current fashion dictates. And this surprises him again and again, that there is so much emphasis on outward appearance in this country, that even people over sixty obey its dictates. There must be countless variations lately in which the colourfully striped scarves are tied around the neck, although with most of them the original purpose – to warm the wearer – has been lost to mere decoration. Höller recalls his attempt a few days ago to tie his scarf in a similar way, which he undid immediately after he had accidentally seen his reflection in the foyer mirror of the small *pension* where he has lived for several weeks.

In front of a closed shop, whose display window is filled with horrible, tasteless pottery, he smokes a cigarette and imagines how visitors from around the world squeeze through the narrow alley during tourist season, hurrying quickly from being amazed by the Piazza to being amazed by the cathedral, then storming into the shops. They gather up ceramics with symbols of the *Contrade*, kitschy watercolours, wild boar sausages and truffles, with the same enthusiasm as Armani jackets, Furla pocketbooks and Gucci ornaments, then they descend with all their junk into Pasticceria Nanini, which must not be missed because Nanini's daughter is a singer and the son is a racing driver. In such a place even the sweets may cost more, but one more or less consumes them anyway, along with devouring the proximity of two world-famous stars, because such an opportunity does not present itself every day. Only a few of them notice the fact that the memorial plaque, on the wall of the house of the city's most important poet, has been tarnished by the weather. And to those who do not miss the plaque, the name means nothing. It is not worth noticing, they think as they walk on, because if it referred to a celebrity, it would hardly be in such poor condition …

Höller tosses the cigarette through a grating and moves on. He is irritated that he has squandered his time with this senseless idea, of hordes of tourists who waltz through all the cities in the world and, in addition to their money, leave behind an equal amount of devastation. Too little time remains for him to waste it with draped scarves and shops full of kitsch.

On the steep steps down to the Piazza his thoughts are once again concerned with the piano recital at the Palazzo Papesse. He had been sitting with Sophie in the second row, on a seat from which he could see the pianist's hands fly over the keyboard. He has forgotten the pianist's name already. A young Italian, not without talent, technically savvy, dynamic in his runs and clear in his attack. A young man with the figure of an athlete and a long black mane, which he has tied into a bushy braid at the back of his neck. A pleasing appearance, which certainly impresses most of the female concert-goers and disconcerts their companions for a moment …

Höller is served *caffè doppio* outdoors at the Café Palio. The waiter asks if he really wants to sit outside in this weather, and returns inside shaking his head. Once again he has let himself be distracted by matters of minor importance. He has not attended the concert because of the pianist, but only because of the hall in the Palazzo. It is important to find the ideal place for the *Fantasy*. After he decided on Castelnuovo, this visit to the concert only served to confirm his decision. Because of it Höller is convinced: for every work of art there is an ideal place for it to be presented. To display *David* in a place other than the Academy in Florence would be the same kind of non-sense as moving the *Palio* from the Piazza del Campo. And one must experience the ultimate interpretation of the *Wanderer Fantasy* in Castelnuovo. After such a performance, it could not be played anywhere else.

Has the second half already begun? Sophie's tired glance when she communicates her decision to forgo the two "Impromptus" and the "Sonata." Why did he lure her out of the *pension* and drag her here, when he must know that she does not regard piano music with the same enthusiastic fanaticism he does and that the cold dampness harms her frail lungs? A question he was unable to provide an answer for, because there was none. At least none that Sophie could have understood. And after all these years of marriage, in which they had continued to grow further and further apart, his silence was enough for her. She did not try to persuade him to stay, nor did she ask a second time for his reason, saying only that he should wait in the Café Palio for her phone call. She would pick him up in a taxi after the concert.

Höller enjoys the view across the oval of the deserted piazza. The noise from La Mangia does not bother him, neither the voices nor the soft music. From time to time people come out of the restaurant to smoke a cigarette. Then they stand in a group outside the entrance, laughing together, and Höller envies them for a brief moment for the collusion that connects them. But while he waits for his second *caffè doppio*, that feeling fades away, because this evening it is no longer true. No longer true in his life, in which there is no room for things that have nothing to do with the *Fantasy* and its ultimate interpretation. How easy his life has become, in one fell swoop, after all the small goals have vanished from his horizon. Yet only one remains. And Höller pities the people in front of the restaurant, those whose lives are surely disrupted by requirements, desires, hopes, and disappointments until only fragments remain, those who attempt to join together in celebration. But the next morning they will wake up under the debris, and the same play will begin again. The waiter comes to his table, and the laughing people in front of La Mangia disappear into the restaurant.

Is he Signor Höller? The Signora is waiting for him in a taxi on the street behind the piazza.

As the taxi heads for the ring road and the driver accelerates, Sophie grasps Höller's hand. She looks at him in silence for a short time, then whispers that nothing has been decided yet and that he could still reconsider his plans and recognise his mistake in time to avoid a serious error that he would be unable to correct later. Höller is silent, and Sophie releases his hand. He really must think about the future of the children. Even if he has taken less and less interest in his children these past few years, they were still his children. He was still responsible for them. He cannot live as if he was alone in the world, free from all obligations …

Höller is silent, and Sophie says she will fly back the next morning. In a few days she must begin the trial that the media has declared will be the trial of the year, in which she will defend a high-ranking politician who is suspected of corruption. This senseless journey, whose single purpose was to find the ideal place for a Schubert concert, has cost her valuable time in which to prepare her case. Now she must read the file again, working day and night to make sure she does not lose the case on the very first day of trial. And after a long pause: perhaps she could understand his reasons for this absurd search, if only he would talk to her. But he has remained silent for months, evading her. The fact that he has lost all interest in his work did not escape her. At first she thought that he was overworked, searching for regeneration in the music, that afterwards he would return his full attention to business. For weeks, no word, until he had announced to her almost as an aside, that he was going to sell the business to the Russians. And this at a time just shortly before admitting that the negotiations were almost concluded.

Sᴏᴘʜɪᴇ ᴅᴏᴇꜱ ɴᴏᴛ ᴡᴀɴᴛ to go into the *pension* immediately after they arrive at Castelnuovo. If he is tired, he can go on ahead. She must take a short walk in the fresh air, to clear her head for the trial. There is more at stake than just victory or defeat. If she succeeded in saving the Minister from a conviction, this case could make her practice one of the top firms in the country. In addition to the prestige, negotiating a favourable outcome for the politician would also expand her circle of well-paying clients. She would hire new lawyers and, in addition to the main areas of criminal defence and divorce suits, could also think about taking on business cases.

When Sophie opens the door of their room in the *pension*, Höller is in bed with his eyes closed.

Are you asleep? Sophie throws her coat over the back of the

armchair, puts her shoes beside the bed and goes into the bathroom. Through an open door Höller watches as she undresses, tying her hair up with a ribbon and stepping into the shower. He sees white skin as if through a film of fog: outlines only, never her entire body. Under the covers he begins to rub his penis. Timidly at first, then harder, but the ridiculous piece of meat between his legs will not grow erect. Despite the great arousal; certainly a reaction to the painkillers, thinks Höller.

You're not asleep! Sophie stands naked in front of the bed. Very little light enters the room. Höller sees water droplets glistening on her skin. She has combed the wet hair at the nape of her neck. He is still holding his limp penis. Sophie turns off the light in the bathroom and lies down beside him. She will leave the *pension* early in order to catch the first flight in Florence. But she trusts him, Sophie says before falling asleep, she has trust in his common sense and his sense of responsibility. And during the days of the trial, she says, it will be difficult for him to reach her, but he should leave a message at the office when he comes to his senses.

HÖLLER IS STANDING at the parlour window of the small *pension* and looking out at the piazza. What fog!

Not uncommon this time of year, says the fat landlady; the autumn haze is most persistent. The retired professor has dozed off behind the *Corriere*.

Should I play a record? the landlady asks.

Höller nods without turning away from the window.

Schubert?

Certainly, Signora Carmela, Schubert!

Painstakingly the woman cleans the record, even the cartridge. A bright crackling. With the beginning chords of the

Wanderer Fantasy the professor wakes up. She will purchase better equipment, says the landlady, like the one in the bar at the piazza. Without those disturbing scratches in the background.

Don Cesare comes out of the bar and staggers past the church.

Will he read the mass this afternoon? Höller wonders.

What gives you that idea? the professor laughs. He is going into the sacristy, to sleep off his intoxication. His afternoon inebriation.

Is Don Cesare really drunk?

Absolutely, says the professor and returns to reading the *Corriere*.

But he is a good priest, says Signora Carmela. The best who has ever read mass in Castelnuovo.

Despite the rumours! the professor shoots back.

Rumours? Höller asks, looking at the professor.

Maliciousness! Unsustainable nonsense! Planted by Communists and Socialists! With a devastating glare the landlady silences the man.

Just rumours, he says, and buries himself in the *Corriere*. Later, when Signora Carmela disappears into the kitchen, the professor comes back to the topic of Don Cesare, saying Höller has understood that talking about the priest is not welcome in this house. So Höller would not hear from him that it is said Don Cesare presses himself on the village youth, the altar boys and the girls from the church choir. He would not tell Höller that the Priest had been found in the vestry with a naked altar boy on his knee. If you want to hear things like that, perhaps with all the details, then you must go to the local Communist party headquarters!

In the bathroom Höller discovers things that Sophie has forgotten: her shower gel, which she takes on all trips, a hairbrush, and a bottle. He opens it and with his eyes closed, he smells the familiar scent for a few seconds. When he begins to imagine Sophie, he opens his eyes again and throws everything into the little bin under the sink.

The memory is like a dog that lies down wherever he wants.

Take an umbrella! the landlady calls after him as Höller leaves the house. If you get caught in the rain, you will get pneumonia.

He does not listen to her and cuts across the piazza with the *Fantasy* in his head. In front of the grocery store, a limping old man drags a sack of potatoes. Höller sees that every step brings him pain, and thinks that at least he is spared from that. He does not have to fear the weakness and the diseases of old age.

In the bar, he sits down at a table with old men who watch him out of the corners of their eyes. As he orders them a round of *Grappa* they put their heads together, whispering and hesitating. Then one of them accepts the invitation, while the rest nod together in agreement.

To your health! Höller learns that they are from the farm.

Farm hands?

Are you crazy? At our age? The farm has not produced anything for a long time. The owner has converted it into a retirement home.

Höller orders a second round. The men drink silently. Then their spokesman asks if he wants to apply for a room at the farm. It is not possible at the moment. There are no free beds. But Giuseppe has not left his room for months. He would probably die soon. After this sentence Höller winces and orders the next round, although most of them have not yet emptied their glasses. After Giuseppe's death, Höller could apply for his bed. He could count on their support. The men drink and nod to him. They must now make their way home. If the weather permitted, he could always meet them at the bar in the afternoon. Then they would report to him on Giuseppe's condition.

AT THE SMALL post office Höller is given stationery. The clerk watches from his counter while Höller stands writing at a high desk.

Is it possible to send a letter from here to England by special delivery?

Certainly! the clerk says and states the price.

Dear *Maestro*, Höller writes, I have finally found the ideal performance space for the *Fantasy*. A few kilometres outside Siena in a landscape that will create a unity with the sounds and rhythms. In whatever direction I look, perfect harmony … Daunting preparations still lay before him. There exists no suitable hall; the community hall (degenerate Mussolini architecture!) was unsuitable, must first be transformed according to musical criterion. The landscape is ideal, but lacking in incidentals. There were not even suitable ushers in the place … But he will sort out these inadequacies in the shortest time once he has the Maestro's consent in hand. Had he received Höller's previous letters? Höller writes; and if it was possible that they had not found their way to him? After all, post office conditions in this country were not the best. The money for the *Fantasy*, Höller assures in conclusion, will not fall through, because after the sale of my business I will have substantial resources.

It is not often that a letter is sent abroad from this post

office, says the clerk. And to England, by airmail, at that. Is Signor Brendel a relative?

He nods, and the man sticks stamps on the envelope.

Höller crosses the piazza. The *Wanderer Fantasy* sounds in his head, the Salzburg recording, November 1971, and drowns out the dull pain. Behind the church, the hill on which the city centre lies falls away abruptly, a low wall extends up to the parish hall. Höller walks along beside it to the rhythm of the *Fantasy*. A few children watch him and later run, imitating his movement through the piazza.

Signora Carmela waits for him at the door, asks if Höller would like a coffee. It would only take a few minutes. Then she complains about the fact that he does not listen to her warnings. She has already told him that he must take an umbrella ...

Has a letter arrived from England?

No, not an English letter, not a single letter this morning, she says, and goes into the kitchen.

Höller hangs his wet jacket on the radiator and sits at a table across from the sleeping professor, where he can observe the piazza.

Italy is a utopia! exclaims the professor when he wakes. An idea of utopia that was already doomed to failure because the politicians are corrupt crooks, which their criminal nature tried to conceal by the fact that they imitated respectable politicians. He throws down the *Corriere* and continues to talk in his usual tone. Words could do nothing to stop the failure. He had withdrawn here to assure that he did not become an accomplice.

No politics in my *pension*! the landlady tries to calm the man down. Think of your heart! No excitement! No politics!

The politicians in this country reminded him of the son of one of his colleagues from the high school, he whispered to Höller after a short break, the only difference being that the boy came to a terrible end, while the politicians, always grinning, fended off all attacks. The two-year-old son of a mathematics and physics professor had become an impersonator, even though no one in the family had given him this idea. Before he could even walk, he imitated everything that appeared in front of him. Voices, gestures, intonations, noises, animals: nothing was safe from his impersonation. He even tried to imitate objects.

The parents were afraid the boy would become a freak, and attempted to distract him from his inexplicable addiction. They bought toys, read books out loud to him for hours, but they did not achieve the desired result. In the end they resigned themselves to the situation and supposed, based on the singularity of the child, that there was an artist in the boy.

When visitors came, the boy would thrust himself with his imitations into the centre of attention, and most of the guests who frequently came to the colleagues' flat would think up a new challenge for the *artist* before their visit.

The boy imitated snakes, bears, chickens, presidents, cars, trees, electric stoves and more. If he could not solve one of the challenges right away, he locked himself in his room until he dared to present his interpretation to the guests.

A mathematician from Viterbo, who wanted to discuss a tricky mathematical question with the mimic's father and wanted the nuisance out of the room for a while, announced, immediately after his arrival, that what he suggested this time would be a difficult task. The boy might try to portray a golden eagle.

Child's play, laughed the artist of mimicry and climbed on a chair in front of the open windows. Before the two men could prevent it, the young boy spread his arms and rushed out of the window. The colleagues' apartment was on the ground floor, and the boy merely broke an arm. But shortly afterwards, when the two mathematicians bent over the child, they saw that he was dead. The shock after the injury had killed the child, the pathologist pronounced. But the father believed that it was disappointment over having failed so miserably as an impersonator.

AGAIN THIS DULL pain in his right temple. The pressure, which Höller has almost grown accustomed to these last few months, is drowned out by a pounding and hammering, even though he has increased his morning dosage of painkillers. He dissolves another tablet in mineral water to accelerate their impact. And then the pain begins to migrate from his head to other parts of his body, seeps into his neck and shoulders, presses into his ribs. Later, shortly before he lies down on the bed, it slices its way into his bowels; Höller draws up his legs, lying on his side and then on his stomach, breathing heavily and waiting until the tablet starts to work and he will fall asleep.

The piazza is filled with old men. They stand huddled together and stare at the church door, in which Don Cesare appears. Only with the utmost difficulty can two naked altar boys support the drunken priest. Their skinny bodies seem to be illuminated in a white light next to the black robes of the priest. Kneel down! he orders, and the men obey, breathing heavily at his command. Crutches and walking sticks clatter against the plaster. A breathless moan falls across the piazza. Every head visible has some deformity. Egg heads, flat heads, water heads, angular heads ... You must no longer stumble through life with your disfigured heads! the priest shouts and orders the men to rise. The Master has answered your prayers, and sends you rescue. Thousands of hats fall from a cloud above onto the piazza. The old men grab them, put them on their heads, adjust them, throw them to the ground and reach for another. They use the hats to flog themselves, beat each other with sticks and crutches. There is hardly anyone who is not bleeding from a head wound, while caps continue to fall from the sky at breakneck speed. The men are now up to their knees in hats and cannot move from the spot. Soon, the men can no longer be seen. Don Cesare pats the altar boys on the buttocks and pushes them in front of him into the church ...

Bathed in sweat, Höller wakes with a start and goes to the window, looks at the empty square and opens a casement. The damp air chases away the images of the nightmare, and his pain has fallen below that threshold to which he has now become accustomed.

No, says the postman, no letter has arrived for you from England.

Keep your eyes open! Höller says as he takes his leave, slipping the man a fifty Euro note.

Castelnuovo sits on two sprawling hills, whose slopes are planted with thick vines. Vineyards, a few craftsmen, several shops with food for daily needs, at the edge of the village a manor that has specialised in sheep farming. The ideal place for the *Fantasy*, Höller thinks on the way to Felsina farm.

The rest home is situated on an elevated point from which the entire city can be viewed. In a display case in front of the community hall, a poster announces a meeting of the delegates of the province and the mayors from the surrounding areas. A discussion of environmental devastation and the sale of land to foreign investors. Following the political component there will be a folk music group from Gaiole with a guest appearance by the harmonica virtuoso, Beppe. An opportunity, Höller thinks, to carefully examine the interior of the community hall. He can check the acoustics and evaluate the changes needed. Apart from the exterior, because Brendel would never play in this building, constructed during Mussolini's era.

As he approaches a young woman with a baby carriage, he recalls Sophie's allegations in the taxi: they are still your children!

What a ridiculous sentence to come out of the mouth of a prominent lawyer. He could invest his entire fortune in the *Fantasy*, and Clemens and Nathalie would still be able to lead normal lives with the proceeds from Sophie's firm. Clemens, the calculating careerist, will join the firm after completing his law degree, and Nathalie will continue her studies in America. She has taken sociology, political science, journalism and art history in the last few years, never passed exams, but, as she informed him this past summer, her personality would mature more fully than would ever be possible in Europe. You got to know influential people and see the world with different eyes after years in America, and with an expanded horizon …

So what would happen to these children, *who are also his*? Clemens' future seems secure, and should Nathalie abandon her attempt to broaden her horizons and find self-awareness in America without results, Sophie would finance a boutique for her or employ her in one of those foundations that her firm managed. Neither of them is dependent on a specialised factory that provides the parts for air conditioning systems to the German automobile industry. Clemens would even now sell it to the highest bidder and Nathalie would annihilate the company's assets in the shortest time by turning the business into a playground for her social romanticism and esoteric daydreams.

An avenue of cypress trees along the ridge leads to the farm, with sloping vineyards on both sides. Through a heavy iron gate Höller enters into an oval clearing, surrounded by more buildings, whose former agricultural use can still be recognised. In the clearing he sees some of the men from the bar, who, despite the damp weather, are throwing *bocci* balls. After each toss they discuss its quality loudly and what is required of the next throws. The next player reaches for his ball only when they have agreed.

When they spot Höller, they put their heads together and whisper, as in the bar. Then their spokesman comes up to him and pushes him into the arch of a doorway. He says the administrator and the doctor would be reluctant to see strangers at the farm. Visits must be announced and approved. Besides, Giuseppe's condition is unchanged; they cannot estimate when the bed will be free. And, above all, we must not put a coffin outside the door of the living. As the proverb says, he adds, when he notices Höller's perplexed look. He reassured the old men that he had not come there because of the bed but wanted to have a look at the city from a higher position.

Then, the old man says, pointing to the edge of the forest with his hand, the best way to go is this direction. From up there you can see everything. But in this fog ...

THERE IS NO one sitting in the drawing room except for the professor.

It is a disaster, he wails, and folds up the *Corriere*. Everything falls apart, and we watch passively.

Höller is silent.

Are you familiar with the history of Italy? he asks.

Mainly with the history of music, Höller says. He has not been interested in politics for a long time.

But the history of music is also political, insists the professor. All sounds are political.

He must go to the post office, he is expecting a special delivery letter from England, Höller says, breaking off the discussion.

Music history! whispers the professor, and begins to leaf through the *Corriere* again.

In the bar, the men at the counter are talking about the event at the community hall. None of them pays attention to Höller, who leafs through the *Repubblica* at a corner table. They should not sell any land to foreigners, yells a bald headed fellow. The Germans and the Swiss used their money to buy up every bit of land they could get. They know well enough who needs the money, and are only waiting until the owners will have to sell.

Höller uses a short silence in the room to order a *caffè doppio*. He is promptly greeted by hostile looks.

The proprietor turns up the radio, which is playing a Tuscan folk song. After he has served the cup, he tells the men at the bar that Signor Höller is a friend, whereupon the men no longer pay attention to him and again talk about the meeting.

Pollini will give a concert in Zurich, Höller reads in the culture section of the *Repubblica*, Chopin, Beethoven, but not a word about whether he will also play Schubert. Don Cesare comes into the bar and orders wine. The men make way, and the priest assures his support for them as he empties one glass after another at breakneck speed. It is not to the church's liking that all the land falls to strangers, who only build hotels and apartment houses where moral decay prevails. Free love, rape, drugs and atheism spread throughout these houses; an Italian brothel is the same as a monastery in comparison with these hell nests. Applause on the counter, where Don Cesare orders drinks for everyone. As well as for Höller, who calls Salute! to the bar, but no one notices him. The red-faced priest announces that he will address this issue in his Sunday sermon, and the men promise to attend the mass. *Viva l'Italia*! Don Cesare roars and staggers out to the piazza.

INSTEAD OF THE long awaited letter from England, the post office cashier hands Höller a fax message from Sophie, in which she complains that an incompetent manager in his factory is making decisions that harm the company. But how can a farmer's son from the Waldviertel region be director of technical operations! You have been warned before about making this country bumpkin the director. And you have ignored all objections with the absurd claim that a man who came from a landscape that represented the ideal setting for Schubert *Lieder* would also be the ideal candidate for this post. She could not see any connection between Schubert *Lieder* and special components for air conditioners. Give this country farmer free reign as director for another few months and he would bankrupt the operation.

Sophie had despised the man from the moment he stood shyly behind the maid one morning in the breakfast room, obviously completely impressed by the mansion, which was still burdened at the time by substantial mortgages due to the necessary expenses and the expansion of Sophie's office. Had the young man known that, he would have certainly discarded his embarrassment in the hallway. But he stood there in front of the breakfast table with downcast eyes, wearing a threadbare suit in the traditional style of his region, holding a hat in one hand and the newspaper containing the job announcement in the other.

Whereas Höller, from the first moment this lost man had entered the room, felt sympathy for him, Sophie's eyes reflected pure rejection. Nobody who is applying for a leading position in management comes dressed for the first interview like the mayor of the last cow town, stuttering from excitement and insecurity and, in addition, is named Unterloibnegger. This was not a name for a factory director, Unterloibnegger, and Höller remembers how Sophie stretched out the name again and again with pleasure. Murderers or child molesters are called Unterloibnegger … And Sophie never forgave the man, because he continued to wear the traditional costume long after he was able to afford Armani suits.

The brown dress suit was too big for the young man. It looked as if he had borrowed it from a relative for the interview. A laughing stock! Sophie whispered to him over the breakfast table and demanded that he throw the clown out immediately. Two, three minutes had passed, and they must have seemed, Höller thought, like an eternity to the applicant. He stood there, red-faced, looking back and forth between his shoe laces and the table, until Höller finally ended the comedy and invited him to sit at the table. Have you already had breakfast?

The young man, who was desperately looking for a place to put his hat, shook his head, and Höller told the maid to bring another place setting. Sophie abruptly put her coffee cup down and left the room, after giving Höller a withering look.

Now the applicant unrolled the newspaper and took out his certificates of examination, which he handed to Höller, who saw that he had completed his studies at the Technical University with the best grades in the shortest time. Did he have experience in running a business, Höller asked, whereupon the young man looked down and whispered that he learns quickly and takes advantage of every opportunity that offers itself to him.

After the *country bumpkin* was hired, Sophie did not speak a word to him for days, a proof to Höller that he had made the right decision. And that Unterloibnegger, even after years as director, wore his traditional costume at official events, and did not drink Barolo but beer from his hometown brewery, made him, in Sophie's eyes, a *non-person*.

A COLD EAST WIND sweeps across the Piazza del Campo. While Höller thinks about the latest tests at the university clinic, an ambulance races towards the piazza with sirens wailing and blue lights flashing. Paramedics carrying a stretcher run into the bar. Höller leaves his outdoor seat and follows them, positions himself in a cluster of people at the bar, where there is someone lying with a deathly pale face. Höller concentrates more on the events at the bar, his memory settling on the very point when one pushes his head one last time into a tunnel, in order to take those final pictures of the head's interior, after which any doubts were ruled out.

A medic leans over the prostrate body, opens the jacket and shirt collar. The radio is playing a sentimental hit from the sixties. Nobody thinks to turn off the music; everyone is watching the person lying on the floor, who dies anyway before the end of the song. Resigned, as if he were to blame for the death of unknown people, the paramedic straightens up and closes the man's eyes with a casually executed movement of the palm of his hand.

After a few moments of shock all of the guests talk in confusion, as if to calm themselves down, while the dead person is placed on a stretcher and carried into an adjoining room. The paramedics return to the counter and order coffee. The owner gestures away nervously over their cups and negotiates with the two of them. The death of a man in a bar just causes the owner problems, an official investigation, unpleasant questions. Having police in the bar ruins the business ... Then he places a one hundred Euro note between the paramedics' cups. You could claim that the death occurred on the way to the hospital. It wouldn't hurt anyone to say the death occurred in the ambulance.

That is not a problem, the older one says after a short glance at his colleagues. The owner places two shot glasses on the bar, the paramedics drink and leave the bar with the dead body. In the bar stories about death are now being told by the guests; talk about a long lingering illness, about accidents and death from sudden cardiac arrest. Why, thinks Höller, doesn't anyone report an inoperable brain tumour? And, even though the mood of the bar grows better from story to story, everyone having already forgotten the dead man, and, if not forgotten, have nevertheless replaced him with their own stories, Höller leaves the bar in disgust. He goes off through the narrow street to the Piazza Matteotti, thinking about everything that they told him in the hospital, accurate findings translated from an incomprehensible professional medical jargon into a generally understandable language: his prospects estimated with numbers; the final date fluctuating between one and two years; each tumour has its own unpredictable momentum, which cannot be generalised; pain killers and medicine for improved circulation; exact dosages determined, which should not be changed arbitrarily …

What had begun as an unexplained fatigue, a logical consequence of his excessive workload, had grown after some weeks into a headache, which only attacked him at first if he worked for hours at the computer screen, and later died away, after he had left his office and run for a little while through the city park. He stepped on the gravel path, heard the crunching under his shoes, which he produced with each step, and after a few minutes reassured himself. When he passed a couple sitting on a park bench, closely intertwined, and they did not notice him, he felt something like confidence and afterwards he was a little more relaxed as he drove to the mansion on the outskirts of town. He listened to Schubert in the car, as always, when he had regained his composure, the "Rondo" from the *Sonata in A major*. Because the evening traffic had already subsided, he arrived before the end of the *Rondo*. He continued to sit in the car, listened to the piece to the end and thought on the way into the house about spending the evening with Sophie. He then wanted to talk about things that concerned her: her current cases, her successes in the courtroom; he was even willing to talk about his children, although they had become more alien to him each year and he no longer tried to understand them anymore, because at some point he had resigned himself to the fact that Clemens was a ruthless careerist and Nathalie a hopeless dreamer. Sophie should determine what they talked about, he decided, when he hung his coat on the rack. He wanted to refute her allegations that any air conditioner in a Mercedes was more important to him than she was, but when they sat across from each other, talking became an agony, and both took refuge in activities that excluded the other.

A short time later the headaches could only be suppressed with strong painkillers, which he easily obtained with a prescription from his family doctor. But after a few weeks the doctor refused to write him a permanent prescription and demanded that he let himself be examined by a specialist. It is not enough to suppress pain; one should find out its cause, in order to initiate treatment. Reluctantly Höller visited a neurologist, who referred him to a diagnostic clinic and advised him, a few days later, when he studied the recorded CAT scan, to visit the university clinic for final clarification. He himself was not ready to issue a diagnosis, because, allegedly, in his facility he did not possess the equipment necessary to carry out the required evaluations. What a coward, thought Höller, when he finally had certainty.

None of the medical authorities who examined him told him how easy it was to die. He should take the unknown person from the bar as a model and think, not about the end, but about the *Fantasy*. And hope that Sophie learns nothing about the diagnostic results.

THE COURTYARD OF the farm has been abandoned by humans Höller sees, as he opens the iron gate. All the windows are closed; the shutters are drawn over most of them. In the sand he recognises the impressions of bowling balls, as if someone had still been playing in this place a few minutes ago. But none of the old men appear, not even at one of the windows. Without knowing what he really expected, Höller walks aimlessly back and forth between the buildings for a while. Later he stands in a dark store room, filled with agricultural equipment. Broken poles, rusty ploughs and harrows, shovels and rakes in a rundown state, indicating that they have not been used in a long time.

What are you doing here?

Höller flinches. In the open door stands a stranger with a Herculean physique. He wears a large, checked flannel shirt; on his massive head sits a Ferrari-red sports cap, which he has drawn over his forehead so that his eyes disappear under the peak. Höller thinks the man is a replica of that brain surgeon who had dared to offer the first accurate diagnosis, and begins to laugh. The giant's head twitches; the veins on his neck stand out. Höller attempts to explain his intrusion but the man does not listen to him, roaring alternately the words *property* and *criminal*, whereupon Höller tries to calm him, and therefore takes a few steps towards him. The man continues to roar without pause, grabs a broken rake handle and swings it over his head like a club.

Höller retreats into the barn; the giant follows him step by step, now crying that he is the administrator responsible for the place, that he will not see any scum hanging around the farm. He is looking for a way in which he can pass by the administrator to reach the outside, climbs over cars, crashes through ruptured barrels, stumbles and gathers himself up again, but the roar comes closer and closer. He hears the heavy wheezing and the threat that he will beat him into a pulp. Then Höller finds a wooden door that he can push open. Through it he reaches a chicken coop in which the animals flutter up hysterically, begin to cackle like crazy and jump in confusion. The furious manager is less than a metre away. Some of the chickens run through a gap in the wall to the outside. Höller throws himself on the floor, filthy with chicken manure, and scuttles after the animals. He looks back and sees the red-faced administrator staring through the hole.

With difficulty he gets up, smeared with chicken shit from head to toe. As long as his breath lasts, he can continue to move forward. He feels his racing heart pounding against his skull, and remembers the last discussion about the test results at the university clinic, where his doctors impressed upon him the need to avoid any unnecessary exertion. For what reason? he ponders, after he has seated himself on a mile marker and now breathes regularly again. Probably not because it could cause damage to his *health* ... Without success he tries to rub the dirt from his clothes with damp tufts of grass. He cannot return to the *pension* in this state. He would become the laughing stock of the children who were always lingering around the piazza. And what would Signora Carmela and the professor think if he came into the parlour in this condition? Höller paces up and down between the vines, faster and faster, in order to protect himself from the cold. He walks for hours before he dares to make his way back.

THERE IS NO ONE IN THE PARLOUR except the professor, who sits in front of the television. With his myopic vision, he buries himself in the *Tele Giornale*. He does not notice me, Höller thinks, and enters the room with his shoes in his hands. He tiptoes behind the professor. Only a few more steps will put an end to his embarrassment.

Look at this! the professor shouts. The daily disaster!

A pity, Höller whispers.

A pity? repeats the professor. Are you still thinking about your music history? About Schubert and Beethoven, while we are dealing with tragedies here? He screws up his eyes and translates the minister of foreign affairs' speech about the airport in Kabul. I understand your minister, Höller says, he speaks a very nice Italian.

Are you still talking about the way things sound? On the television screen the weather forecaster announces a high-pressure system and beautiful weather. I have not offended you? the professor asks. And a little later: Why do you look like that?

A fall, says Höller, trying to appease him, a harmless fall in the fog. And he remembers, as the professor turns again to the television set and no longer pays attention to him, a childhood friend of Sophie's, who descended in just a few months from being a respected scholar to a town drunk and troublemaker.

After he had not seen him for months, Höller met the Germanic studies professor Kölz in the reeking toilet of the Augustinian Cellar, where he was trying to pull himself up with both hands on the edge of the sink. A single punch had split his upper lip and had thrown him to his knees, the dead drunk Germanist scholar groaned, and ran his tongue over the wound. Blood, a desperate kind of tiredness and no trace of the stranger with whom he had offered to engage in a fight. In order to clarify his own position in the world, every man must seek out confrontation with others. Since he was no longer invited to academic conferences and his wife had left him, Kölz missed this possibility, which he hoped, with varying success, to rediscover in the bars. Disapproval, artificial fights, jokes, and only rarely a serious argument in which he always left it up to his unknown opponents to propose the subject under dispute. Because the subject of the debate is not important to him; he is only concerned with the dialectical process, but after this preamble most of the bar's guests turned away, disgusted or bored with him. For this reason he had followed the unknown person into the toilet. After all, one can carry on a dispute there just as well as in the restaurant; dialectic has nothing to do with ambience or odours …

Can you manage on your own? Do you want to file a complaint …

Kölz stood before the tarnished mirror, pressed a handkerchief against his lip and reassured Höller: No police, no commotion; if perhaps he might have a band-aid … and a glass of red wine. He would not wish to cause any disturbance in the wine bar's business; he is only concerned with converting people in his situation, abandoned or left behind, into individuals with whom he could carry on a debate, from which both parties would gain the strength to continue.

Later, after the bleeding had stopped, the owner had rinsed the glasses, the restaurant had emptied and only a few hopeless drunks sat at one of the rear tables, without paying attention to whether or not Höller followed him, Kölz told his story:

I SAT OVER A stack of seminar papers on the poetry of Expressionism, and observed with disgust that the students never think of anything I have not already read in books and essays. I swam in self-pity when I thought, while I choked down the choppy sentences, about being pushed to the sidelines by the academic senate. A buffer-stop at the end of a pair of rails and no way back to the main track. But this, as I am always telling myself in order to calm down, just leads to absurdity.

For I had found a way to help reconcile myself with the

failure, but when I thought of my much younger wife, all my confidence vanished. Then I felt my failure twice, and the defeat was something I was as ashamed of as an abnormality everyone compulsively stares at. Again and again I smelled my wife's small perfume bottles, looked in the mirror, my young wife beside me, and my despondency was unbearable.

I know how whores and Madonnas smell / After a movement and mornings on waking / And to the tides of their blood, I read in a thesis on the early poems of Benn. Its author pursued abstruse theories about the relationship between body and mind, between physicality and the ability to think, so the student wrote, and cluttered his sentences with the whole stagnant garbage of philosophical anthropology. He had not digested the mind-body problem. I corrected and did not notice my wife, but when she placed her hands on my shoulders, I looked up from the work.

Time takes its toll against inactivity, she whispered without introduction into the silence, and I did not know what she wanted to say to me. I was silent, from perplexity on the one hand, but also because of the unfinished work on my desk. He who neglects his body, confines his thinking! I wondered what she wanted to communicate to me with this sentence, which reminded me of the regurgitated philosophy in my student's work. A reference, perhaps, to the fact that I fought for years unsuccessfully against my excess weight?

She had discovered the first signs of developing cellulite on her thighs, said my wife, and slipped out of her pants, stripped off her stockings and pressed her index fingers against the area above her knees. She turned around and talked about depressions and striations, while my eyes clung to the well-known curves that I could never give up. She had enrolled in a fitness studio, would struggle and not make time's battle an easy one. She is not yet ready to be defeated by the years …

Her sentences did not make sense to me, as little as the sentences in the seminar paper. She disappeared into the bathroom. I followed her, one line from Benn in my head: *The sweet loveliness clings to me like a film on the edge of the palate.* All of a sudden I felt old and imagined my young wife in this fitness studio, restrained by gleaming chrome equipment with which she expanded and compressed her muscles. I saw her taut skin, her body, which she stretched in a room filled with muscular and well-proportioned individuals. I also saw the tiny drops of sweat on her forehead and the looks from men when she bent her legs or spread them against the weight of the machine. With each of these visions I grew smaller, grabbed myself by the hips, felt soft flesh that bulged over the waistband of my trousers, stroked my flabby cheeks and double chin.

While she turned her back to me, I tried to identify the depressions and striations which she had talked about, groped, examined my own legs and disgusted myself by my powerlessness. In the lecture halls, I surprised myself with the realisation that I was glancing at the legs of the female students and comparing them with my young wife's legs. If I saw a woman in a short skirt, I looked for depressions and striations and became more despondent with every glance. While my wife attended the fitness studio, I got drunk in a student café.

After a few weeks the owner asked me not to come back anymore. The women were bothered by my glances. And again a few days later I read a short story about a Peeping Tom, posted on the Institute's bulletin board, written by that student whose work on the early poems of Benn had stated that a neglected body leads to a decreased ability to think …

AND ALTHOUGH this evening had a poor outcome, Kölz said as he took his leave from Höller at the plaza in front of the wine bar, he would continue to pursue his project to present himself as an opponent for debate to lonely and abandoned individuals.

FROM THE SMALL library next to the radio set in the parlour, Höller takes a narrow volume: Malerba, *Salto Mortale*. He skims through it for a bit and then reads: *THERE IS NOTHING HERE. On the map every object has a particular character and each piece of land a first and last name, but nobody knows anything about it. Sometimes on the map it is called Holy Mary of the Water Heater or Madonna of the Late Arrivals, St. Mary of Impotence or St. Kaspar of the Buffaloes, but why exactly Buffaloes? There are so many animals in this world, and I have never seen buffaloes in this area. Or it is called Heart Quarter, Broom Quarter, Massimetta Quarter, but where are all these quarters? I have never seen them and never heard of them. I look at the landscape all around and see nothing, there are no signs on the ground …*
    While Signora Carmela polishes the espresso machine and turns her back to him, Höller asks: Are there any buffaloes in Castelnuovo?

IN THE BAR the old men from the farm sit and carry on a toothless murmur. Höller does not understand any of it. By chance he hears one word clearly. It is a word from the regional dialect that he does not know. Have they heard about his encounter with the administrator? He orders brandy for everyone; a few raise their hats and caps into the air and toast him. Then their spokesperson comes to his table and says he has no news for him. Giuseppe's condition was unchanged. He does not leave his bed any more, but that did not mean much at his age. At the moment there is no prospect of the bed, but they would keep him informed of any change.

No, says the postman and stood up, rises now with out-stretched arms behind the glass counter, no letter has arrived from England. That would be a sensation, an English letter, general delivery to his office. And when he detects Höller's disappointment:

The English letter has probably not arrived yet because weekly service at the post office throughout the country is provided according to regulations. *Sciopero bianco*, you understand?

Höller nods, puts a twenty Euro note on the counter for the man and leaves the post office.

Hours before the start of the event Höller stands in front of the community hall. The glass doors at the main entrance are blocked. Gray concrete surfaces; he does not see a single window, only round glass bricks just below the flat roof, like the portholes of ocean liners, the only passage for light. He presses his forehead against the glass door. The lobby is blurred in a diffuse twilight. At the back there is an open wooden door. Probably the entrance into the hall, whose dimensions he cannot imagine. But this much is certain: Brendel would not play in such a dreadful place! The community hall must be torn down to the foundation and rebuilt before the concert. A new concert hall, which could also be used by the municipal-ity for its meetings. Which would give the place this advan-tage: the Mussolini rubbish would disappear from its centre and a building with superior acoustics would be erected. The renovation is simply a question of money. And if the community must take part by making a symbolic contribution to the costs involved, resistance is not to be expected. It would be by far more difficult to establish the concert hall in another place. Since there is no property available in the centre of town, they would have to do without a central location. But to choose an outlying area meant taking a risk. Could a concert hall be built on a precipitous vineyard? Do acoustics suffer beneath the vines? It is also impossible to move the construction into the lower valley. The fog and haze that gathers between the hills there lasts for months. It would press against the roof from above and cause chaos. If Brendel did sit at the grand piano under such circumstances, you would not be able to distinguish him from a gifted piano student and he would be surprised by the sounds that followed his chords. He would think it was a conspiracy and would threaten with lawsuits; the disruption would be perfect, the *Fantasy* would have failed before the first note.

A truck stops at the side of the building. Two men jump out of the cab, walk along the loading area and pull up the back of the tarpaulin cover. One of them climbs into the truck and hands the other one stacked plastic chairs, which he places beside the tailgate. White, red and yellow chairs with armrests, like the ones found in all the beach cafés in the Mediterranean. Unfit for musical purposes. A concert hall with plastic chairs. As colourful as a cheap trattoria. Plastic and concrete choke sound. The *Fantasy* would be suffocated by these materials. Hopelessly destroyed, even more so than in the countless unfortunate interpretations.

THE HALL WILL only be open a half an hour before the event!

A dwarf in gray overalls stands beside Höller. It is pointless for you to wait in this weather. Have a coffee in the bar. Out here you will simply catch a cold.

Are you the person in charge? asks Höller.

I have the keys and clean the town hall, says the dwarf. Although he wears a quilted leather cap, he only comes up to Höller's chest and, when he speaks to him, must lean his head far back. His Adam's apple protrudes like a dancing walnut.

Is there any possible way to take a look at the hall before the meeting? Höller slips the dwarf a bill. The dwarf takes his greasy cap from his head, pushes his free hand through a crop of hair, slicks it back elaborately and replaces the cap. He does not know whether this is allowed, there are no precise rules ... Höller offers him a second bill. The dwarf snatches at it tentatively.

You must know I'm personally employed by the Mayor. And only from him did he receive his orders: errands, shopping, gardening, transactions of all kinds. He looks around and asks Höller to follow him inside. From the lobby they end up in a room where, at the narrow side in the back, a stage has been built. With a long table and chairs. Later, the dwarf explains, the political representatives and the dignatories will sit there.

Höller imagines a shiny black Steinway on the stage, which Brendel cautiously approaches. Sweeps over the wood a few times with the flat of his hand. Sits on the bench and fishes a package of Elastoplast and a pair of scissors out of his coat pocket. He cuts small strips from the adhesive bandage; carefully adheres them to his fingertips. A final look, then Brendel's fingers pounce on the keys ...

And how do you like our community hall? asks the dwarf, who is suddenly standing in front of Höller with a broom and shovel. He has to clean the floor. When the politician comes to Castelnuovo, absolute cleanliness must prevail.

For a first visit, Höller says, perhaps he has seen enough. He will come back on another day when there are no politicians in the hall.

Come along! the dwarf calls after him and sweeps the floor.

BACK OUTSIDE, Höller imagines the dwarf as an usher. The black uniform with gold braid shall make the deformed man an authority, one who will not tolerate any rebellion and will squelch every insurrection with his squinting gaze, emphasised by an ominous, dancing Adam's apple. But he will not be able to buy the uniform readymade.

Höller walks to the piazza. More than four hours before the meeting begins. The political bigwig will already have made the journey, sitting in the back of a black Lancia and studying the press reports on the parliamentary sessions of the last week. How did the journalists react to his speech? Do they quote one of his colleagues for his remarks? Does the chairman of the party advance their position? Then he reads letters from his constituents, all written in clumsy sentences and always with the same requests. Can't you drive any faster? As you command, *Onorevole*, whispers the pale driver.

The *carabinieri* drive past Höller in their blue Alfa at a walking speed. The passenger in the front seat looks at him briefly, then the car accelerates and races on toward the centre of town.

While the rushed politician in his Lancia skims through ridiculous letters from his constituents, his wife attends a cocktail party in a Roman palazzo. Female politicians speak about opera and theatre, about fashion and holiday destinations. They stand during the spiritual dignitaries' questions and answers, pay homage to an irrefutable Catholicism, until a Peruvian Cardinal promises a private audience with the German Pope, which they find *terribly chic*. They are handed off from the Church to an arthritic *Commendatore*, who wants to explain the outlines of the Italian policy from Scalfaro to Napolitano to them. They speak in his direction, while their eyes cling to the tight-fitting trousers of the liveried waiters. My husband is on the way to his constituency, the politician's wife whispers and follows the waiter, to whom she slips her business card while she reaches for a sparkling wine glass. Just at this moment, the politician in his Lancia is reading a letter from an abbot, Höller imagines, in which, quoting holy scripture, he complains that in direct proximity to his monastery a brothel is to be established. The city council had given its consent; only an order from Rome can keep the brothel away from his monastery walls now. Faster! The pale driver presses the accelerator, the politician lets his body sink into the leather upholstery and falls asleep.

In front of the *pension* a boy blocks Höller's way: Signor Brendel, do you have a cigarette for me?

THE PROFESSOR STANDS at the window and looks out at the piazza, saying he would also go to the community hall this evening and see the political representatives. The *Onorevole* above all.

What a fine word for a scoundrel, he says, and sits down again at his table with the *Corriere*. This noble word is the wrong choice for the title of a job! Which will be confirmed during the evening's performance. The so-called *Onorevole* and the mayor are now playing theatre. They will bring *Commedia dell'Arte* to the stage of the community hall, which will include all the elements of vulgar, impromptu plays: vanity, ill-fated love, envy and jealousy, violence, threats and insidious conjuring tricks. A *furioso* to common vulgarity ...

Höller thinks only about how he can flee the room without exciting the professor even more. Signora Carmela is out shopping. Only her return could silence him. So, Höller, because he hopes to cut short the professor's inflammatory speech, says that the whole of life is a comedy, and with this sentence brings the man into a rage again.

Spare me your platitudes! he shouts. Through images from the art world I try to show you the difference between reality and appearance, and you answer me like a farmer from the village. You shatter a painstakingly designed edifice of ideas with a single cliché! Inadequate, Signor Höller! Go to your room and think about my pictures! Or listen to your *Fantasy*! Imagine your Franz Schubert at the piano with his thick fingers, and hum the melody!

The stereo is still packed away in Höller's room. He will not set it up until he has found a house. And he sets a deadline of a few days to find a suitable property. He will not haggle over the price. The landlord will receive what he demands. He takes his pain medication. As a precaution he increases the dose, in order to keep from being surprised during the event in the community hall. Then he drafts a letter:

Dear Maestro, I visited a possible performance venue early this afternoon. A responsible person, (an obscure phenomenon!), with whose description I would not like to trouble you, led me through the so-called community hall, adeptly, but with obvious uneasiness because of the unusualness ...

Höller abandons it and crumples up the sheet, because he

has nothing concrete to report. He will write to England again only when he has new information.

Barely one hour until the event. Höller showers and shaves carefully. Later he picks the dark suit from the wardrobe, ties his tie and examines its exact placement in front of the bathroom mirror. *Land for sale to foreign investors.* This theme is also of interest to him. Feeling is directed against him. It will be difficult to rent a house in Castelnuovo where he can prepare the concert without disturbances. For weeks the regional papers have been stirring up sentiments hostile to foreigners. He must keep himself in the background without attracting attention. One last look in the mirror reassures him: he looks like an underpaid teacher or a minor bank official.

Join me! the professor shouts to him from the piazza. Are you also going to the event?

There are groups of people standing in front of the entrance.

Look at that! the professor says. Everyone here is old. Maybe a few are middle-aged. Young people do not interest themselves in the country's problems. Young people sit on their motorcycles and all they think about is the fastest way to get to the big cities. It is not important to them who lives in the vineyards and country houses, because they can no longer endure the view. No money, no entertainment, no life, the young people think, and have already started their motorcycles.

While the professor continues to condemn the youth with his clichés, he does not even notice that Höller has long ago ceased to listen. He is thinking about his children. He wonders whether Sophie has informed them of his plans or has waited, because she still hopes that he will abandon them. Nevertheless, she probably thinks that he is overworked and the *Fantasy* project is only an idea that he hoped for a short time would let him escape from the daily grind. Clemens would not oppose the sale of the factory to the Russians, but since all of the money from this business is going into the *Fantasy*, he would have been horror-stricken to find out about the reduction to his inheritance. And he is probably thinking about how much he will lose when he projects the interest rate with the average statistical life expectancy. Nathalie would have only been interested in whether or not the sale affected her monthly allowance. If this was not the case, she would see an individual possibility in the *Fantasy* project, liberating his personality from a hopelessly frozen way of life and initiating an expansion of his horizons.

In the meantime the dwarf, in a threadbare suit and the greasy leather cap, has stationed himself at the entrance. His head is constantly in motion, observing every new arrival. And although he does not speak to anyone, his Adam's apple hops up and down at a frantic pace. When he spots Höller, he quickly tips the brim of his cap and immediately looks away.

You know Gesualdo? asks the professor.

Höller nods.

A fascinating biography, the professor says. Southern Italians from an impoverished family of farmers. His childhood, an unknown variable, but certainly the usual: a family with many children on a dilapidated farm somewhere between Lecce and Taranto. Stony soil, withered crops. Oppressive debt to one of the few large estate owners. And the result? The professor asks and looks at Höller, who is silent. Violence! the professor shouts so loudly that the bystanders stare at them inquisitively. These looks do not bother the professor. He continues to talk, barely quieter. Violence, until the law intervenes. Gesualdo was arrested, placed before the court and condemned. No one here knows the reason. Except the Mayor, who took him in after his release from the prison in Volterra. It is clear that it must have involved a blood crime, but no one will take any interest in it as long as Gesualdo is under the Mayor's protection.

The doors are open! says the professor, seizing Höller by the arm and pulling him toward the entrance. Loud folk music can already be heard in the lobby, whereupon he whispers to Höller, this is not a lobby, but rather limbo. Meanwhile, most of the visitors have gathered in groups and talk to one another. The fact that no one observes him and the professor, who will not leave Höller's side, calms him down. In front of the platform there are large terracotta pots with dark-green bushes that are as high as the tabletop.

Are you thinking about the purpose of bushes? asks the professor. You may believe that the pots were placed there for decoration? That would be a huge mistake … At any event you go to where there are politicians, you will always find protective greenery, because the politicians in this country are as vain as anyone else. Completely effeminate and stuffed with bribes, their bodies out of shape. If the scallywags stretch out their soft, bulky, and bloated bellies to the audience, after the first glimpse it would mean a tremendous loss of authority. So the politicians conceal their bellies behind optimistic greenery. And the reassuring effect that emanates from the colour green should not be underestimated. The politicians can say whatever they want and nobody will rebel, because the shrubs stand between them and the audience.

Höller cannot shake off the chatterbox. The folk music group on the stage plays one Tuscan folk song after the other. Höller sits beside the professor, off to the side, in one of the last rows, where no light falls from the stage. Slowly the hall fills. Then, a fanfare. The mayors of Radda, Gaiole, and Castellina are presented by the Mayor and take their places at the table. The politician appears last, a scrawny old man, who, because of his size, is leaning forward slightly.

Look, the professor whispers to Höller, how they have to hurry to hide their bellies behind the bushes.

But not one of the men on the stage is overweight! Höller contradicts.

Deception and self-control! the Professor shouts, and a few visitors from the front rows turn around. He forms his hands into a cone and now talks into Höller's ear. Of course they were fat, even infinitely fat. But for the short distance from the door through the hall to the stage they would figure out a way to conceal their bellies. A technique of self-control taught to them at seminars in the academies of their party, because the partics long ago recognised that they cannot do anything with politicians' heads. They are useless, desolate receptacles for the placement of hats. Sooner or later they all end up like my unlucky friend, who, until a few years ago, taught at the most important university of Rome.

For more than a decade the professor of Roman law sat over his work, with which he intended to become one of the preeminent legal scholars. He concentrated his whole life on the work in which he thought about fundamentally new, even unheard of (as he indicated at times), ways to bring light to the different forms of slave emancipation. During the many years of research, without his even having noticed, first his two children, then his wife, left him. Since all his relatives lived in the south of the country and he had not found friends apart from his research, he now sat in his department like a hermit.

He loved nothing but his papers. Many thousands of closely described pages, which he arranged repeatedly in new stacks on his desk. He thought about his future life; he imagined resounding success, which he wanted to achieve with his final book.

Like children who are often smothered by their parents' immense love and are driven to failure, the almost completed research began to suffer under the great lunatic hope that its friend placed in it. It felt as if with every day it was coming closer to completion, it lost more of itself, while the professor greedily absorbed its loss into himself and expanded with every research result.

It thought only about with whom it could ally itself against the professor, as it had known for years, that Roman law had no use, except to make life difficult for professors and students.

It could expect no help from the assistants, who, in their dependence on the professor, ate from his hand. It was not even capable of escape from the Institute. It could only save a man who had not worked with Roman law. But people disinterested in the legal system did not come into the room very often. It was in despair, when it remembered the heavy cleaning lady who came early in the morning, before the professor went to the university, to clean the Institute.

For days on end the work collected the energy to cast itself, one Tuesday morning shortly after three o'clock, from the table to the floor. The cleaning woman, thinking that it was waste paper, burned the work in the small furnace that the professor had set up as a backup to the central heating, because he came from the south and suffered from the Roman cold the entire winter.

When the professor learned the truth after several day-long

investigations, he attempted suicide, but failed, because he was familiar with Roman law, but not with the simplest medical concepts. Crazy, but for his environment perfectly harmless, he withdrew himself after that to his parents' house in the south of the country.

While the mayor tries laboriously to familiarise the audience with different aspects of the discussion topic, the professor falls asleep. His head has fallen to his chest, and sometimes he gives off a heavy snoring. The mayors report on their towns, enumerate how many houses and how much land has already fallen into foreign hands, quote figures and skim through statistics on the table. In the back the politicians talk to the members of the folk music group. The mayors are silent; individual words from the musicians can be heard throughout the hall; more people leave, returning to their places soon after with full wine glasses.

One should not be opposed in principle to the fact that foreigners settle in the province, says the Mayor, and Höller listens. He talks about the economic importance and the money that they bring to the communities. He also talks about one record producer, who owns a castle, where visitors and artists from around the world frequently stop, spending large sums of money in the businesses and restaurants of Castelnuovo. The politician nods, jots down a few words and then begins to speak. About the history, the beauty of the landscape, tourism as a major economic factor. By and by he moves away from the general remarks; more people get wine glasses from the lobby, which does not disturb the speaker, because this way the presentation can end with a mixture of folk music, alcohol, and vague statements. With a pathetic *Viva l'Italia*, he finally finds a conclusion, and the band begins to play. The professor is still asleep next to Höller, who leaves the room assured: It will not be impossible to rent a house in Castelnuovo.

PEOPLE CROWD in front of the post office, but the cashier leaves his place as soon as he discovers Höller at the end of the line.

Unfortunately! he shouts in a volume so loud that everyone who is waiting can hear him.

Unfortunately no letter has arrived from England today. And, directed to those who are waiting: for days we have been waiting for the English message.

Höller pulls the man a few steps away from those who are waiting and asks him to speak more softly. It was embarrassing for him if everyone …

Of course, the cashier says again, so loud that everyone listens in. He understands. The English message is their secret and not intended for the general public.

IN THE BAR Höller drinks coffee and skims through the newspaper without interest until he discovers in the local part of the *Giorno* a small story that was probably only there in order to avoid empty space: *Expensive funeral – After a serious accident on the Autostrada between Fano and Forli, the right foot of the truck driver Giuseppe Benarrivo (42) from Ancona had to be amputated below the ankle. Usually, amputated limbs end up in the hospital's hazardous waste container. Following an old superstition, that after the death of the patient the separated limb would grow back again and the dead person would enter the other world intact, Benarrivo insisted on the burial of his foot in the family grave. The funeral home calculated the costs for cremation and ceremony at 2,000 Euro. Many relatives and friends attended, but no priest. The amount is equivalent to a conventional funeral. No reduced costs are provided, the managing director explained, for partial burials. The funeral oration was given by Benar-rivo's passenger, Carlo Tozzi, who emphasised, in moving words, the reliability and precision of the foot in the daily protection of highways and city streets. The urn was placed in a concrete niche in the family tomb to Puccini's "Sola, Perduta, Abbandonata." And despite the painful loss, there was good news in the end for Giuseppe: a shoe manufacturer from Varese announced that he would make a special shoe for Benarrivo, so he can continue to practise his profession.*

At the bar, an official from the *carabinieri* is talking in a low voice with the owner. As he leaves the premises, Höller buys a pack of cigarettes and asks for directions to the record pro-ducer's castle. It was impossible to miss the castle, the owner calls after him into the open air.

From the piazza he sees the farm on the opposite hill and the group taking the cypress-lined alley up toward the main street. Today he will not waste time with the old men. He leaves the main road and goes through winding streets behind the piazza.

They will not discover him here, because they always take the shortest way from the farm to the bar.

Television voices from open windows. It is a game show that housewives especially like to watch. On the football field there is a school class in colourful tracksuits running their laps. With shouts and shrill tones of his whistle the teacher in the middle of the field regulates the speed of the children. For a while he watches the children, then he continues and comes to the road to Gaiole, which will take him to the castle in one quarter of an hour.

Höller follows the high wall up to the wrought-iron gate and is disappointed. The castle, in his mind a palace, differs from the other cottages only by a bay window, dominated by a tower on one side of the roof. So he cannot be seen from the property, Höller leans against the wall beside the gate and thinks he must find a similar house in which he can concentrate on his preparations. Then he skims through the steps that lie ahead before the final performance of the *Fantasy*. The purchase or rental of a home guarantees a smooth sequence of preparations. In that regard, he hopes for a useful recommendation from the record producer. Negotiations with the authorities on the reconstruction of the community hall into a concert hall. For this, he must obtain the consent of the Mayor. If the renovation is completed, it must be examined by Brendel. And what happens if the result does not meet his requirements? A delay? A severance of relations?

A few steps further Höller feels that he has reached a critical point in his deliberations. He sees Brendel go into the re-designed concert hall, the eyes behind thick glasses constantly in motion. An indignant shake of the head before he pulls a tuning fork out of his jacket pocket and strikes it on the podium. With eyes closed Brendel hears how the standard pitch slowly fades away. Again he shakes his head: Schubert cannot be played in this caricature of a concert hall!

Sophie enters from an alcove and walks toward Brendel with a superior smile. She apologises for the discomfort of the journey and the accommodations; this had to end in a fiasco. Brendel nods agreement and no longer pays attention to Höller, who sees the Mayor coming toward him from a darkened part of the hall. Close behind is Gesualdo, cap pushed down over his forehead. And although Brendel's annoyance grows weaker with each of Sophie's sentences and he now smiles again, the Mayor and Gesualdo are getting closer and closer. Höller hears Brendel's voice from the side: he will not remain in this place an hour longer.

Fraud! the Mayor yells from the front, and his deformed shadow nods in agreement.

The *Fantasy*! A few corrections, adjustments, acoustic interventions, technical refinement, very common problems in other words, no reason to leave and to pitch the *Fantasy* into the debris of the demolition! Höller calls after Brendel, who does not respond and moves towards the side exit with Sophie.

Within an hour the helicopter that will bring him to the airport for his flight to Florence will be on the piazza. In less than five hours he could step off the airplane in London. Everything is already planned, Sophie soothes Brendel, who nods absently, his thoughts returned already to England.

What are the Mayor and Gesualdo planning? In Höller's head the *Fantasy* begins to sound. *Allegro con fuoco ma non troppo*, but what is the progression of notes? Becoming ever softer, the *Fantasy* rewinds in his head until it fades with the opening chord. Sophie and Brendel have left the room. As if from far away, the noise of the helicopter engine. Dust whirls into the hall from the open side door, from which the Mayor and Gesualdo now emerge.

Criminal! the Mayor yells.

Höller hears how the word sounds in the hall, and he knows that the tuning fork has deceived them. The mayor's voice returns the proof. He wants to tell the man that it is an unfortunate mistake which can be resolved if someone could establish a connection to the airport in Florence; a short phone call; just a few sentences, and Brendel will return to Castelnuovo.

Silence! the Mayor roars, and Höller remembers what the professor told him about Gesualdo. Remember, tucked under the leather cap is the head of a murderer; tucked into the jacket pockets are the hands of a murderer, which, with one sign from the Mayor ...

Looking for someone? The postman is standing next to Höller with his bicycle.

Is this the record producer's house?

Certainly, says the man, pushing his bicycle along the wall and pressing the bell button on the iron gate. With a buzz the gate opens, and the postman disappears.

A LIVERIED ASIAN PORTER leads Höller into the hall and asks him to wait. The meeting in the studio would not last long. Höller regards the framed concert posters on the walls. All of them are artists whose names he has never even heard, dressed in bright costumes. He sees bizarre hairstyles and absurd looking glasses. To him, they look like the ensemble of a ridiculous fantasy film. With one exception: LAURA. In skin-tight jeans, she stands at the beginning of an avenue of pine trees. Lips slightly open, gazing off into an undefined distance. She reminds Höller of Nathalie, whom he had already begun to consider during her last years of university as his *lost daughter*. And this was not because she wanted to leave the family, but because of her continuing enthusiasm for hopeless projects. An inclination that had already distinguished her during her time in elementary school, and one that Sophie, whenever he anxiously raised the topic with her, regarded as evidence of the child's creative nature. For him, as an entrepreneur accustomed to thinking in terms of austere budgets, it was of course difficult to accept a trait in his daughter, one that requires imagination and furthermore reaches beyond the restrictions that the ABCs place upon a lively child's soul, Sophie reprimanded him, when he appeared to be concerned by the complaints from teachers because Nathalie was neither willing to accept the rules of spelling nor the basics of arithmetic without contradiction. She wanted, for example, to write the word *father* in her essays with both *F* and *Ph*, depending on whether the father in the passage should be described as happy or serious.

The child just thinks more than her peers, Sophie ended such conversations, never without pointing out that it was she who had taken over the main responsibility for the education of the children. After she had won some sensational cases and the press began to take an interest in her, Sophie suggested that they should not leave the training of the children to underpaid amateurs, but to entrust it to private boarding schools, where the personality of the young is holistically developed.

Clemens was sent to a sinfully expensive English institute, where he wrote meaningless letters which always began *Dear Mother*. If he came home on holiday, he predominantly spoke English, which Sophie was thrilled over. Again and again she praised the perfect pronunciation and the enormous vocabulary of the little climber, which was suspicious to Höller at the time. Not least of all because Clemens flatly rejected his proposal to use their native language at home, emphasising the importance of English. He even insisted that Höller must improve his English if he wanted to remain competitive, and volunteered to help him in exchange for appropriate payment.

Nathalie, on the other hand, did not write a single letter, a proof to Höller of her loneliness. Sophie did not consider that a valid observation. She said that the child had found a consistent work ethic in the Swiss boarding school, one which he had demanded for many years. That Nathalie was not reprimanded by the boarding school on several occasions, because he had transferred a large sum of money to the owners, Sophie assessed as a sign of their daughter's strong personality. She had retained her creativity despite all the discipline and the strict rules of her life in the boarding school.

And what do you have to offer me? the record producer jerks Höller from his reflections.

What a character, Höller thinks, and stares at the man without saying a word. Receding hairline, stubble, an enormous stomach behind a silk shirt that is open to the chest and shines in all conceivable colours. The scornful expression does not disappear even as he asks:

Now, what do you have to offer me? Let me guess. You have a daughter, with her delicate voice that arouses the withered feelings of old people? Or a son, who sums up the misery of the world with the notes of his guitar? Or perhaps you yourself have been misunderstood for many years?

What are you talking about? Höller asks.

Make your offer, the record producer continues. We will talk about it, and then you can go away! We will go into the studio. I will listen to your tapes!

My tapes?

Do you like LAURA? he asks later.

Höller is silent.

But you have been staring at her picture in the hall for several minutes. By pressing one of the buttons that are embedded in the back of his armchair, the man starts a tape. Höller listens to a sentimental song, simple rhymes, in which an unrequited love is confirmed again and again. My last success! the producer says with a satisfied grin. A half a million CDs sold in less than a year ...

Amazing, Höller says, wondering how he can bring the discussion around to the castle.

Höller should know that he is indifferent to any kind of music. He is interested exclusively in the commercial aspect, and this worked well, as long as his birds were singing on every channel ...

Have you been living here very long? And how have you enjoyed the castle? Höller interrupts him.

You do not want to palm off a singing daughter on me?

How did you find the house? Höller asks.

If you want to buy something in this area, contact the lawyer Panella. Without him, absolutely nothing happens here. His office is located directly behind the plaza.

On the way back, Höller hums the refrain from Laura's song, trying to imagine the singer between the pines.

IN THE REAR PART of the bar there is an old jukebox that is rarely used, because the radio on the counter is usually playing. But the guests only listen to it on Sunday afternoons if the football championship games will be broadcast. Then the men stand around at the bar with their football betting slips filled out and calculate their chances of having guessed the correct thirteen this time.

Chiesa and Vergassola are injured, so Lazio will win.

But the referee comes from Turin. He will know how to prevent it!

Scarcely two hours of tension, then the dream of easy money fades and a round of grappa is ordered.

Höller is looking for LAURA on the jukebox chart, but

even after the second reading he does not find her name. After tossing a coin into the slot he pushes two keys at random, whereupon the tremolo voice of a crooner sounds. His tearful song vanishes into the noise created by the old men from the farm as they enter. Without taking off their jackets and coats, they squat in the front part of the restaurant. They put their heads together and squint again and again in Höller's direction. Höller signals the owner, who places a tray with glasses of grappa on their table.

Unfortunately, nothing new! says their spokesman. Giuseppe has left his bed and he is now eating with us again in the dining room. Since the fog withdrew, he has gained new strength. He even talks about women and his virility. He is always talking about the women with whom he … Giuseppe's thoughts always circle around a single point. If we talk about lunch, he talks about women. We are very happy that he no longer talks about death, but about his daughter-in-law.

His son has a wonderful wife, Giuseppe says. When they visit him at Christmas, he imagines her naked. Or he watches with his eyes half closed as she undresses. The red hair fallen to her breasts, her tiny panties stretching across her bottom. Later, she bends forward a little, so he can inspect what hides between her thighs. He would really like to jump into bed, but she talks about the grandchildren. Her son is studying medicine in Padua, she says, with brilliant success, the doctorate in sight, she says; the daughter, philosophy in Bologna, with brilliant success, she says; while he looks at the hair tossed against her neck as she climbs into his bed. Too bad that they only visit him once a year …

Again and again he shows them an article that he cut out of a magazine, the old man continues, a yellowed and crumpled piece of paper, from which can be gleaned, in the year 1889 at a meeting of the Biological Society in Paris a well-known physiologist stated that an aqueous extract prepared from the testicles of dogs would not only increase male potency, but also cause an erection in completely impotent subjects after only a few injections.

Höller orders another round and hopes that over the grappa the old man would forget his absurd story. But he has barely emptied his glass. He continues to talk, and his companions, who almost always crouch in the bar with an absent gaze, hang on his every word as if they are also hearing the account for the first time. Whenever we go to the farm from town, Giuseppe asks whether we have met any women. Then we bring him joy and say, we have seen them in droves, women of all ages. We tell him about a young waitress who wears a short black skirt that slips up when she stoops, and Giuseppe is satisfied. What do you think, Signor Brendel, does Giuseppe's article give us hope?

Höller is silent. He does not want to set the men against him and then he supposes, when he notices their expectant eyes, that he is not very well versed in medical matters, but if something appears in an illustrated magazine, it will probably contain an element of truth … He immediately sees a contented smile on the men's faces.

And who will procure the juice from the dog's testicles? someone asks. With his asthma he cannot run after a dog; Giuseppe, with his wooden leg, was too weak; Andrea cannot manage it because of his epileptic seizures; Franco because of his shortness of breath … At the farm there was only the administrator's dog, and he wasn't going to let anybody near his balls. The young assistant nurse makes out with the administrator;

he saw them disappear into the administrator's office while the hound from hell crouched in the corridor in front of the locked door, guarded it and licked his pink member …

Our problem, says the old men's spokesman, is the dog. There is no safe way to get to the dog's balls. In any case, before the juice is extracted from the testicles, the dog would have to be drugged. Either the dog, or we will never again in this life lie between the legs of any woman!

A few guests at the bar laugh, and Höller considers how he can make a bolt for it without annoying the men. Even before he had found an excuse, the old men's spokesman speaks again.

When, on a walk through the farm, he observed a bull mounting a dull-eyed cow in front of him with a mighty snort, he began to cry. But then, when the steaming bull slipped off of the cow again and again and finally gave up, creeping away with a hanging head, he had laughed out loud, roared with laughter, so hard the assistant nurse had asked whether or not he felt okay.

The bull seemed like an ally to him, says the old man, the bull's incessant slipping off reminiscent of his last attempts to penetrate a woman with his flabby dick. Inside a worn out whore, one he had spoken to in the early evening in Fiesole. A dirty slut who stank of cheap booze. Of cigarettes and rotten teeth. But he had gone the whole hog. He overcame his disgust and offered the drunk far more than she had demanded. He had taken a room in a lousy *pension*. For a quarter of an hour the woman stood under the shower. But that was little use. Even then she still stank. One cannot wash away the odour of years from the skin and from the body in one quarter of an hour. Naked, she stood with hanging breasts in the middle of the room under the lamp, counted the bills and smiled. Then she was crawling on the bed, a flower-patterned bed sheet with semen stains and blood, settling on her back with her legs spread. He had already feared, with a side glance at the woman, who had now begun to groan awkwardly, what occurred a few moments later. Despite all the efforts of the prostitute, who squeezed and sucked with her toothless mouth, throwing herself into her work come hell or high water. It had all been in vain and he was not able to penetrate her. He fared like the bull in the pasture, but in contrast to him, the bull at least had achieved an enormous erection …

There are currently no prospects for the bed. And do not forget: we must not put a coffin outside the door of the living!

He regrets not being able to help, the hotel manager says and backs away like a stooped ninety year old with gout, until he pushes against the door and excuses himself one last time. Höller is at the window and because of the pain, he has wound a wet towel around his head.

Hotel porter! he shouts into the next room, but Sophie does not reply. Money-grabbing hospitality-riff-raff. In Florence, not the slightest difference exists between the Savoy and a cheap hourly hotel in the area around Santa Maria Novella. The staff circulated through the house like decorated Swiss Guards, but the manager was not able to find any concert programs from recent years, so he could not figure out whether or not the *Fantasy* had been played in the city in the recent past.

The absurdity of the so-called *first-rate hotels*! Copies of the old masters on the walls, a Veronese over the toilet tank, but no archive of concert programmes! Remember the *Imperial*, when the waiter had served us the dessert, accompanied by a mighty belch? What use was the apology then, in perfect French? Do you remember this belcher from our anniversary?

Sophie was silent. Höller looks at the Piazza della Repubblica. The images are blurred; the houses seem to move as he tries to fix certain points. But just as he has focused on them, they swim through his vision, and he tries to find evidence of the next one, with the same game repeating itself. The brain specialists have referred to the possibility that during the course of his disease sudden visual disturbances can occur, whose duration could not be estimated. At any rate, he should avoid driving a car in the future. The doctors' concerns no longer applied to him, Höller thought at the time, but to those people he could kill by driving. And what a strange sound the word *future* had when they related it to him.

WHILE SOPHIE RUNS the bath water Höller leaves the suite and goes into the hall, where the employee at the reception desk draws his attention to the towel: A minor ailment, Signore?

Everything is all right, Höller calls out to him. The towel and the headache!

A boy points a finger at him and is dragged away by his mother. Children! she apologises, with a heavy southern American accent.

At Café Gilli young people sit around outside in jackets and coats, their collars turned up. And of course you also find the artfully draped scarves here, Höller determines, but tonight he steals the show from the other fashionable arrangements of fabric with his towel.

The waiter with the thin gold-rimmed glasses, who looks like an impoverished aristocrat among the guests, helps him out of his coat and asks if he should take the towel, too. Höller shakes his head, and the waiter takes his order. As he brings the chocolate to the table, Höller asks about concert programmes, whereupon the man hands him an event brochure that he leafs through quickly. Later the waiter wishes him a speedy recovery while helping him into his coat.

Is Sophie sleeping already? If she is not sleeping Höller knows that she would want to talk about the proposed business deal with the Russians, and after the unexpected pain he had little ability to counter-attack her arguments. With the sure-fire instinct of a star lawyer, she would press him into a corner with a few specific questions, from which he could no longer escape. He would have to confess, and Sophie would know, as if she had studied the experts' findings like she studied the files of her court cases. In this case, the ultimate interpretation of the *Fantasy* would be in extreme danger, if not aborted. And Höller, while turning at the square in front of the Dome, tries to imagine how she would react to the unexpected clarity. A first shock would very rapidly be replaced by practical considerations, Höller assumes, as he stands in front of the baptistry and tries to focus on the figures on the golden doors. He continues to be disappointed when he finds that his condition has hardly improved. He would no longer matter; the children would come into the game again, Höller presumed, those regrettable children, whom he robbed of their inheritance with a crazy project. Or would rob, unless a court order declared his understandable but still intolerable insanity. His complete incapacity, as it was probably called in legal jargon, which can have only as a consequence that he would be declared incompetent and incapacitated. Accordingly, the most obvious thing for any court to do would be to transfer the guardianship to Sophie, who could now prevent the *Fantasy* project with a single signature.

Another cognac? The waiter fills the glass without waiting for a response from Höller, who is imagining Brendel at the grand piano, his glasses with the thick lenses pushed to his forehead. What if Sophie is already sleeping? Like the *Fantasy*, because he is not making any progress with his preparations. The alcohol does not dull the pain in his head as he had hoped. It was a mistake to leave the pills in the hotel. From now on he will always carry them with him, Höller thinks and looks back at Brendel, who is adjusting his glasses. The *Fantasy* was created in the Autumn of 1822, he explains to an invisible public from the grand piano, and clearly stands out from previous piano works. The fact that he noticed the syphilis for the first time then could be a coincidence. The piano as orchestra ... Then his fingers fall on the keys. The initial chords of the *Fantasy* vibrate through Höller's head and make him forget the pain.

As Brendel gets up from the piano bench, Höller orders two grappas for the drunken soldiers beside him, who empty their glasses with one chug and move a little away from him. After the next glass, they ask about the nature of his headache and talk about diseases in their families. He hears about grandmothers with uterine cancer and fathers with heart attacks; even birth defects and fatal accidents at work. In any case it would be wise to keep the head warm, they say, and then stagger out of the bar. The tourists standing at a high table in the back of the premises have not observed the scene, he determines. Then his eyes fall on the clock. Is it still possible to send a telegram to London?

A few men in cheap suits move closer. A fat bald man orders Höller a cognac. He introduces himself and wants to invite him to join his company of friends, interprets the silence as an invitation and signals to the men who now surround Höller to come over. They are so close that he can smell their shaving lotion. They are travelling salesmen, he hears. Then, from behind, one of them puts a hand on his shoulder. The towel begins to come loose. Höller ties the ends together and pulls it tight again.

We are talking about your head!

My head? Höller seizes the towel.

Or about the pain in your head. Or the type of head injury. My friends and I commiserate with you.

When Höller remains silent, the bald one whispers into his ear. No man slings a towel around his head when he leaves the house without a reason. No man, he repeats, and wraps Höller's head in a vapour of sweat and cheap shaving lotion. Numbed by the disgusting musk of the travelling salesmen, Höller knows that he cannot drive these men out of the bar with a few drinks like the soldiers.

Until a few months ago, Höller says, the ordinary head of a manufacturer sat on my neck. Now and then the hint of Spring fever. Never a serious illness. Eventually, my interest in the business began to wane. For days on end I did not go into the factory, but after breakfast I climbed high up into the attic of the villa. Where I squatted between the spider webs on the dirty floor next to the fireplace chimney. For hours I remained there in the same position, undisturbed, because nobody suspected me to be in this place.

The bald guy orders a round for his friends. The waiter buys a round for Höller, because he is interested in his story. Usually he hears stories about women, failed marriages, wayward children, crime, or football games in his bar. Höller's story is different. It does not bother him if it is invented. The truth is just boring …

After the travelling salesmen have had a drink, Höller must return to the attic. He has not yet provided the justification for the towel. He sits thus under roof rafters and the bricks, says Höller. It is clear that the drunken travelling salesmen will not cease without a story from him. He is sitting in the same hiding place he fled to as a child from the wrath of his father …

Your father and your childhood do not interest us! someone in the group interrupts him. We are interested in your head. We want to learn more about the pain in your head or your head injury! Do not try to foist your father on us as a substitute! After all, you have forced yourself upon us with your towel and we have not forced ourselves on you with our curiosity!

His story is far less interesting than they assume. Höller makes another attempt and sits down again beside the fireplace chimney in the attic. He loses interest in his factory; every day he is less interested in the business. Instead he thinks of piano music, which is not a surprise to him, because he himself had also played the piano for a long time until his father had ordered him to take a course of technical studies, in order to ensure the continuity of the factory in the family. This was indeed from the father's point of view understandable, but for him it meant the end …

You want to distract us with your father again? one of the travelling salesmen barks at Höller, who cannot escape the crescendo of aggressiveness or the fact that the men move closer.

He thinks about piano music, mostly Schubert, Schumann and Liszt, but also a little Mendelssohn, and again and again about Beethoven, from which they could perceive his preference for classical and romantic music. Certainly, a loyalty to the traditional repertoire, but he would argue about musical preferences just as little as he would argue over feelings. Neither of them is a matter of reflection and logical conclusions. After a few days, just thinking about music was no longer sufficient: he also wanted to listen to it. But that was not possible in the usual way, since the music would be heard in the upper floor of the villa and his hiding place would be discovered. So he decided to turn his thoughts about the musical pieces into sounds and save them in his head, where they did not die away as they did in the concert halls, but settled in and did not diminish, even if he started the next piece. The sounds did not replace each other. They forced their way into the interior of his head and gained intensity, which created a huge pressure in his head that made him fear after a few days that his head would explode in a huge cloud of sounds. But even though that did not happen, it was inconceivable to him that such an enormous mass of sound could be stored in a person's head. Admittedly they pressed against the skull and had produced a centre of pain from the archive of sounds that sent their signals to all the other regions of the body. And with the wet towel he was trying …

As Höller looks up from his glass, he notices that the travelling salesmen have left the premises. Only the bored waiter, leaning against the shelf with the glasses.

We're closing! he says, and turns off the overhead lights.

HAS SOMEONE attacked you? asks the postman at the only open counter.

No, says Höller. I want to send a telegram to England.

So no young criminals, who had a go at you?

Is it possible to post a telegram to England now?

Certainly, the cashier says, but Höller knows that he is only interested in the towel.

An accident? A collision with a reckless driver on the piazza? Höller drums his fingertips against the glass counter.

The city is full of criminals and young thugs. The city is ruled by English morals, which one can only by force …

And the telegram? Höller interrupts him. The cashier pushes a form toward him and explains in detail how it is to be completed. For this purpose he pushes the blunt end of the pencil along the lines. When he finally comes to an end, he asks again whether or not Höller had fallen into the hands of criminals. The man has mistreated the form so much that it is torn in several places.

Useless! he says, and that was the last form for foreign telegrams. The others were in a filing cabinet and the nightly service personnel do not have a key. Unfortunately, he could not post his telegram to England until the following morning. The counters opened at eight clock.

As Höller passes through the darkened hall to the exit the clerk shouts after him: he would still like for him to show his head wound before he left the post office. On the Piazza della Repubblica, young people do laps with their mopeds, travelling between the enclosed souvenir stands and the tables of the cafés with howling engines in a slalom of boredom.

ARE YOU STILL suffering? asks the clerk in the *Savoy*. Höller remains silent; he wants to avoid a further conversation about the towel. If Sophie is sleeping? As he goes through the hall to the lift, the clerk begins to speak to him from behind him. He remembers a secret recipe of his grandmother, a true miracle cure for headaches of every type …

Memory, Höller shouts to him from the lift, is like a dog that lies down wherever he wants.

Before Höller pushes the card through the slot to unlock the door, he takes the towel from his head and smoothes back his hair. Sophie should still be awake; he will not provoke her with his absurd appearance. But he also knows that he cannot dodge a conversation about the *Russian Deal*, as Sophie called the planned sale of the enterprise in her last text message, a second time. After all, she has flown to Florence for this reason during a break in her trial. The suite is dim, only a light burning over the vanity mirror in the vestibule. Höller takes a look into the bedroom through the open door and hears Sophie's steady breathing from the bed. He quietly closes the door. He will sleep on the sofa in the parlour, so as not to waken her. But that does not mean more than a brief respite. He has only a few hours left to arrange a strategy. Höller sits at the desk and knows that he cannot find one, because he has set out to conceal his condition. The only hope remaining is that he will succeed in deterring Sophie from interfering with the sale. With her connections, ranging all the way up to her child-hood friend, the Minister of Justice, she would accomplish it, if not to prevent the *Russian Deal*, then at least to delay it a few months. Months that he did not have to lose, if the *Fantasy* is still to be played by Brendel in the time allowed.

On the desk, in a leather folder, Höller finds chronologi-cally arranged newspaper reports about Sophie's trial. Most also include pictures of her in elegant attire in the corridors of the criminal court; in an ankle-length coat in the court parking lot as she rises straight out of her BMW coupe; in her law-yer's robe in the courtroom. For the first time Höller learns what the politician who is absent from the photos has been accused of. He has allegedly taken money for himself and his party from a French company that has received a contract for the construction of several tunnels through the Alps. A *French Deal*, Höller thinks, Sophie is defending a corrupt politician and has negotiated a partial victory through an adjournment in negotiations, according to the unanimous accounts. So far she had been able to instill the findings of the prosecutor with so many doubts and uncertainties about the prosecution witnesses that the judge had no other choice but to interrupt the trial for several weeks. The latest accounts show Sophie's winning smile, while the weak features of the Minister continued to be blurred during the days of the trial.

THE UNIFORMITY WITH WHICH the taxi moves calms Höller. With each kilometre the argument loses acrimony. What a morning at the *Savoy*! Sophie stood in a black trouser suit at the window and looked out at the Piazza della Repubblica, next to the desk a packed suitcase, while Höller, half-dressed, woke up after a terrible night with terrible back pain. He asked for coffee; Sophie pointed wordlessly to the table. With every step he felt stabs against his skull, as if they triggered a dull pressure of pain, radiating out in all directions. Vertigo, which caused the images to vanish before his eyes.

The memory of a video that Nathalie, then sixteen, brought home from her Swiss boarding school during the holidays and showed to all the relatives. The family and friends gathered together in the salon of the villa, to watch a video with the title *I'm floating on the river Limmat*. It was shot during a visit to the Zurich boarding school and not only showed the city, but also reflected her soul, Nathalie said, before she darkened the room and started the video. Everyone present was prepared for a longer show, had supplied themselves with drinks and snacks and tried as best they could to feign interest. In fact, the video did not take longer than three minutes, during which one saw Nathalie, infinitely slowly, cross the Limmat river over a bridge. Actually one did not see her, but rather suspected her, because the school friend who operated the camera was shaking like an invalid in the final stages of Parkinson's disease, so that all those present had the impression that it was a documentary film recording a severe earthquake in Zurich. After the short demonstration, Nathalie demanded that those present discuss the video while under no circumstances leaving out the existential dimension of the film. This request was followed by an awkward silence that Clemens broke with a cynical laugh, by asking his sister if it would not have been possible to mount the camera on a tripod. Nathalie started a hysterical screaming fit and threw a silver candleholder in the direction of her brother, who, however, ducked; whereupon the candlestick wounded the wife of the president of the Bar Association on the temple so deeply that her lacerations had to be sewn up in the emergency room with eight stitches. After this unfortunate demonstration, for a week Nathalie only left her room when she was alone in the villa.

I hear nothing but excuses from you! Sophie screams. I always try so warmly …

Höller covered his ears with his palms. Sophie increased her volume. The waiter for their floor knocked and inquired whether there was a problem. Sophie grabbed a crystal ashtray and threw it at Höller, who tried to catch it, but seized empty air. Fortunately, the ash tray landed on the soft seat of a chair. The shouts from the waiter grew louder. From the suite next door, banging on the wall. The phone rang; Höller lifted the receiver. The hotel manager threatened to call the *carabinieri*. Sophie discontinued her accusations and calmed down a little.

Höller assured the manager that the problems were resolved – there were no more misunderstandings.

She'll fly back, Sophie said later. If he is not able to do it, she would take care of the business, ensuring that everything is moving along as usual …

And the *Fantasy*? Schubert and Brendel do not interest you? Sophie did not answer. She called the reception desk and asked if they might order a taxi to the airport and pick up her suitcase. After the bellboy had knocked on the door, she joined Höller in the bathroom.

When the manager gave him the bill with a regretful smile and supposed that his next visit would be under more favourable circumstances, Höller said that man is a writhing, dismal creature.

A perplexed look and then relief: Your taxi has arrived.

The signpost shows the turn off to Colle di Val d' Elsa, half an hour to Castelnuovo, while Sophie is already sitting over the documents in her office again.

WHAT IS DEPRESSING YOU this morning? asks Signora Carmela, and Höller knows that he must now quickly offer the woman a convincing explanation, because she would continue to talk to him until she had obtained it.

The serious illness of a distant relative, says Höller. Cancer is suspected. The final test results are still pending, but the doctor's indications make them fear the worst. No, Signora, not a young man …

As the landlady takes a few steps toward him, he is afraid that she would gather him in her comforting arms and kiss him on both cheeks. Fortunately, he is spared this closeness. Höller also sees that she is satisfied with his explanation, because in a low voice she tells him about a cousin in Arezzo, who had died from cancer over six years ago. During the last few months he had taken no solid food, and the family no longer looked after him in the house, although the doctor came several times a day. The cousin had steadily lost weight and at the end weighed just over thirty pounds, so that the pallbearers had guided him to his final resting place without the slightest effort.

RELIEVED, HÖLLER NOTES that he is alone in the breakfast room. So he may think about his next steps without disruption. The folded *Corriere* lies on the professor's table. Another table is set. Two elderly ladies from Milan have arrived in his absence, Höller learns from Signora Carmela. Sisters from an influential family, known throughout the country. The brother is a respected politician. Höller cannot focus on the *Fantasy*. He thinks about Sophie, who is already considering the ways the *Russian Deal* could be prevented. He must therefore consult his lawyer, who, as his lawyer, was not allowed to speak to third parties. And if Sophie succeeds in eliciting information from him? Höller considers, and remembers that she had unsuccessfully harassed his lawyer for months with her attentions. How would he react if she made a few little advances on him now? But a business relationship that has lasted for years is not shattered by the uncertain hope of an erotic adventure, particularly since his lawyer will receive a substantial sum by concluding the *Russian Deal*.

The ladies from Milan come into the breakfast room, and he has not yet made any progress in his preparations. Signora Carmela bombards the two with pleasantries and also includes Höller in her performance by asking him to their table and presenting him as a foreign entrepreneur who had dedicated himself to music.

The two look at him intently and then invite him to their table. Höller cannot refuse. He sits opposite the ladies, and has already lost sight of his preparations. The landlady brings an espresso, and Höller is taken by surprise. Smiling, Signora Carmela returns to the kitchen.

While the ladies from Milan stir the sugar in their tea cups and brush butter over their croissants with affected movements, they observed Höller. He thinks in their black dresses they look like wooden beams with heads. After the first croissant, and before they butter their second, they unload the story of their lives on him. Or at least, what they think is important.

You need to know that I am recovering from a complicated operation in the United States, says the one. From a highly complicated bone marrow transplant, the second one adds.

Höller wants to think about the *Fantasy*, and these two are sharing their bone marrow with him over the breakfast table. He reaches for a cigarette case, but before he can open it one of the sisters shrieks. He may not under any circumstances smoke in Viola's presence. It could cause serious harm. And she calls out to Signora Carmela. She would like him to be served a second espresso as compensation for the ban on smoking. Then she pats the back of his hand with her cold fingers. To distract himself from the physical contact Höller thinks of Sophie's skin, but before he can imagine it, the story continues.

You must keep in mind my medical history. For almost ten years I lived in complete uncertainty, between hope and resignation! Whereupon the two sisters embrace in their seats and assure each other that neither one would survive the *departure* of the other. And then he needs to hear all the details;

how the one sister has donated bone marrow to the other; how the healthy one had *sacrificed* herself for the terminally ill one; that the intervention had been a matter *of life and death*; the American doctor was a *true genius* in his field, worthy of being awarded the Nobel Prize; that the brother will also exert himself for her with the *entire weight of his political authority*; even after the U.S. operation weeks of uncertainty in Detroit, until the cathartic diagnosis that her body did not repel her sister's bone marrow ... Can you imagine a closer connection between siblings?

Please excuse me! Höller whispers and leaves the breakfast room. In the narrow corridor he bumps into the professor. Sorry! Then he kneels in front of the toilet in the bathroom, his head on his crossed forearms. He sees himself going through the sales hall of a fish market, animal blood everywhere on the dark tiled floors. And on the wooden tables, where the fat, twitching eels are usually writhing in aluminum troughs, there is bone marrow plaited into braids.

THE WHOLE MORNING Höller lies in bed, exhausted from stomach cramps. Incapable of thinking about the *Fantasy*. The ladies from Milan surface again and again; individual sentences and words cross his mind. They spoke of a ten year period, without suspecting that the time they have left, compared to him, represents an entire lifetime. If he had ten years he would ...

Höller breaks off because, since the last discussion about diagnostic findings at the university clinic, he no longer calculates in such terms. To distract himself from the two ladies, he thinks about the heart attack victim in the bar who, until the seconds before his death, probably only knew the word *deadline* in connection with payments. Around noon he made the decision to leave the *pension* as soon as possible.

Höller walks across the completely deserted Piazza to the post office. Later he will call Sophie, in order to learn from her tone or perhaps from a throwaway remark what her next steps will be. He opens the door. The postman is already running towards him and whispers in his ear, he is inconsolable, but the English letter had still not arrived. Höller is not even thinking about that at the moment, because he has focused only on the phone call, but he tells the cashier nothing about that. Because he does not know how he could have begun a conversation, he quickly leaves the post office and goes to the bar.

He is the only guest. The owner polishes wine glasses and checks their cleanliness against the light from the neon lamp over the bar. In a corner, one of his children sits over a school essay. From time to time he asks his father, who only occasionally answers, and reluctantly, about the spelling of a word. If he is silent, Höller thinks, he does not know the answer and he feels ashamed of it in front of him and the child. Several times he tries to send the boy out to play on the piazza, but the boy insists on finishing his essay first.

On Höller's table there are a couple of newspapers and magazines. He puts these and the *Corriere*, which reminds him of the professor, off to the side. He did not leave the university voluntarily, Signora Carmela reported to him, and probably hoped he would let her in on his own plans when she entrusted him with the secrets of her only permanent guest. The professor was from a noble family and it had not been necessary for him to work as a teacher. From the return on his investments he could have *lived like a prince*, yet he had gone to work in a Liceo and had been trying to cope with the teenagers. He was older than fifty when he married a young woman who had deceived him constantly and finally abandoned him when his fortune had been exhausted. After this blow the Professor had grown odd; he had neglected his outer appearance and had frequently turned up at the university drunk and unwashed. But the decisive factor for his forced retirement was the absurd political ideas which he had recited to his students instead of the curriculum. Only a dirty residue of Italy remained, he stated, a stinking cancer. He had spoken to the young people about the Americanisation of Italy, finally about the Balkanisation or the Africanisation or Japanisation. Finally he had the pupils write in their notebooks that Mussolini and his spiritual protégé Fini are the only upright politicians in Italian history …

In the cultural pages of *Giomo* Höller finds the short story by a young author from Naples, whose title makes him curious: *The Art of Becoming Lighter …*

The engineer Di Matteo feared nothing so much as the evening, when he had turned off his computer in the engineering office to go home. He sat at his computer and worked on a draft. He felt light, although he weighed two hundred and twenty pounds and his nickname Tonnellata was more than deserved. When addressed – again and again he jokingly involved his staff in discussions about his weight – Di Matteo always countered that his body was the only thing keeping him on the ground; were he not so heavy, he would fly after his thoughts into outer space. He never talked about his chronic shortness of breath, the arthritis in his joints, his pathologically elevated cholesterol and blood sugar levels. On his way home he had a tormented look on his face that he attributed to his compromised health and not to the inescapable fact that

Di Matteo would soon sit across from his family and the daily evening disasters would tumble down on him. His wife's reports over her disputes with the neighbours; the claims of the elder son, who had abandoned not only his studies, but who also two or three times a year drove a brand new car until it was worthless; the unfortunate liaisons of his daughter, always culminating in suicide threats, which Di Matteo wished she would finally put into action. The despair of the younger son, who wanted to be a combat pilot in Castro's Air Force, a plan offering no prospects for an extremely short-sighted Italian. The weekly letters to the Cuban president and the commander of the Cuban air force were not even answered. The rate at which the Cubans took up his time, however, and the tearful eyes behind thick glasses spoiled Di Matteo's appetite. He ate just a little more than one plate of soft pasta and moved on to drinking, to balance out his calories, as he explained to his nagging wife if she commented on his repeated trips to the cellar, with the story about an uncle who had miserably gone to the dogs in a detoxification centre. She wanted to spare him this misery, this pain, this indignity, those shivers after a fierce fever, to spare him the tortures of this treatment, she lamented, while Di Matteo uncorked a new bottle.

He thought only of how he could escape from his family for good. Di Matteo knew that just going away would solve nothing. His tracks could easily be followed. After a few weeks, months at most, he would be crouching again in his family prison.

Before making his way to the office on the first Monday after the Christmas holidays, he stood for a long time in front of the tall mirror in the hallway. In the subway, as he occupied one and a half seats and like each day was therefore accosted, Di Matteo had an idea that could turn everything around. Fat Sack, he heard just within earshot, and Pig Face, Hippopotamus and Polpetta,

Dumplings. But on this Monday he did not wince under the name calling, did not try to hide his head under the upturned coat collar.

At the office he began a radical diet, did not have the usual two pieces of cake after espresso and instead of lunch ate just a peeled apple. Di Matteo renounced the Tuscan red wine and switched to San Benedetto mineral water. Between Easter and Pentecost he had reduced his weight by half, and the secretaries in the engineering office let him know that they wanted to take time for him, that they wanted to ensure that he felt good; even his aging wife let herself get carried away with erotic advances, not knowing that for decades sexuality had no longer represented a rewarding subject to Di Matteo. He was only interested in his final flight. His short-sighted son, with his yearning for the Cuban sky, supplied him with important advice. His escape route could not be horizontal; to be conclusive, it must be vertical. Which meant that after the way to the bowels of the earth was barred, only the flight up into the air remained.

From the rooftop of a hotel in Livorno, the emaciated engineer lifted off with a favorable wind, but despite his low weight he flew only a few millimeters. A high-altitude flight was out of the question.

Di Matteo returned to his desk and found the solution. The computer had just crashed and the destroyed hard drive was sending meaningless messages to the screen.

He had to erase all thoughts from his head. It had to be as empty as the ruined hard drive. For days he worked at forgetting. Then he returned to Livorno.

On a sunny Wednesday afternoon, the engineer Di Matteo lifted off from the roof terrace of the Hotel Regina and has never been seen again. The waiter, who claimed to have seen the master engineer fly away, was fired. A hotel like the Regina could not afford to employ a drinker ...

A few pages later, a correspondent reports from Berlin on the collapse of the piano manufacturer *Bechstein*. After a side glance at the magnificent interpretations Arthur Rubinstein had recorded on pianos with this brand name, the journalist explains the *demise of Bechstein* with the effects of the American real estate crisis and the world-wide recession. As if Wall Street would have any influence on the sound quality of a grand piano. The perfect sound of a top notch piano would transcend every stock market crash. The sounds of a piano are more stable than the price of gold and also conceivable as the basis for an international monetary system. This move would revive the global economy.

The words *recession* and *stock market crash* would disappear from the newspapers and only surface as solutions in difficult crossword puzzles. Certainly it would take years for the world economy to adapt to the piano sounds. But this change would entail a further advantage: the politicians and company bosses who were hostile to music would have to resign ... Höller folds the paper and lays it aside. *The collapse of Bechstein,* he says to himself softly a few times. He remembers the professor, who told his students about Japanisation. The quality of Asian piano brands has continuously improved in recent years. Was *Bechstein* the victim of Japanisation?

THE LAWYER'S OFFICE is in one of the old houses that stand on the hill behind the Plaza. Most of the shops behind the tiny windows are closed. Like a labyrinth the narrow streets lead up the hill with several branching forks, all of which feed into a small piazza and finally end in front of the castle wall where the offices of the municipality are. He will also have to negotiate with the Mayor there, Höller reasons, over restructuring the community hall. But first he needs a house where he can arrange the final preparations for the *Fantasy* concert without interference. He walks on and looks for the sign of the firm. He does not see a street sign anywhere; just house numbers on blue plaques. A window is opened on the second floor above the street, and an old woman starts to hang laundry on a line that is stretched between two windows.

Höller asks about the lawyer's office. He must speak louder, she shouts back; she is hard of hearing and cannot understand his whisper. He repeats his question.

Louder! the old woman cries and asks if he has a speech impediment.

So Höller roars as loud as he can: Signora, where will I find the lawyer?

The pigeons on the roofs and the balconies are eating away at your words, the old woman roars back, and Höller moves on.

Signor Brendel, are you looking for the lawyer? Next to him is the boy who has begged from him several times in the piazza. Höller nods, wondering whether the boy is following him. And if he is following him, does he sneak after him out of curiosity, or because someone hired him? But who would be interested in him here?

Give me five Euros, and I'll take you to the lawyer's house! Höller secretly slips a bill to the boy, who runs without a word to him through the narrow alleys and stops beside a massive wooden door with brass fittings. Before Höller can ask a question, he has already disappeared around a corner.

He moves the heavy door knocker a few times, then the door

slips open a crack and a woman's head forces itself through into the open air. Höller can only make out a black headscarf, enormous horn-rimmed glasses and a narrow mouth. He inquires after the lawyer.

What is your business? she croaks out of the door opening.

Up close, he sees that she only has a few teeth left in her mouth. Now he thinks about the lady from Milan and her bone marrow. A sharp pain in his stomach; for a few moments he is unable to speak.

What is your business? the old woman repeats impatiently.

It is a personal matter, says Höller, and the old woman hisses in his direction, to the people who visit her son all matters are personal. She will admit him only when he has described his concerns carefully.

Some of the shutters in the surrounding houses are open. Höller sees that his conversation with the old woman is observed. He wants to buy or rent a house, he says, loud enough for the people inside the shops to hear and not draw any wrong conclusions from his visit to the lawyer. The door is opened; the old woman is dressed all in black and asks him to follow her to the first floor. Höller climbs a steep staircase behind her. Half way she stops and says he has to think carefully about what he wants to tell her son. My son is a busy man who could not waste his time. It would be best if they pause here on the stairs a little and he arranges his phrases, so he would not inconvenience her son any more than absolutely necessarily. Her son has too good a heart, she says as she continues to walk, they do not respect him; day and night there are people at the law firm who beg for his assistance. Only the mother of a lawyer knows that people fall upon him like vultures, because they themselves are not capable of doing anything and needed his assistance in all things. They were called *clients* in the language of the law; one should call them *idiots*, because they needed her son's help in the simplest matters. But she had not raised her son so the idiot clients could suck the blood from his veins ...

Then she leads him into a tiny room where only a little daylight falls through a narrow window. Höller takes the lawyer's seat at the desk; likewise, the old woman sits across from him at the table, scattered with paper, books, pens and files. In between, an ancient telephone whose receiver has slipped off the hook.

On the walls, shelves of books, maps, half-full bottles, flower pots, cups, a plate with leftover pizza. The old woman turns on the table lamp; in its light the law office appears even more implausible.

I will take your name and information about your business! she says, looking for a pen, discovers the phone and places it back on the cradle.

Here! Höller says, pointing to a pencil which shows signs of chewing at the blunt end. She sharpens the pencil with a fruit knife, tears a piece of paper out of a file folder and begins to write.

Then suddenly, without Höller having heard him enter, lawyer Panella appears beside his mother and is hardly taller than her. What a laughing stock! Höller thinks, and cannot grasp that this is the man without whom, as the record producer has remarked, nothing can happen here. A deformed gnome with greasy hair who is in an oversized black suit and looks like he could be the twin brother of the dwarf from the town hall.

The old woman leaves the room and Panella sits in her place. He eyes Höller and makes a few notes. Höller waits for him to begin speaking; he can see from his mother's notes why Höller is visiting.

At the moment it is difficult for a stranger, the dwarf lawyer creaks, to buy land or houses. The uncertain economic conditions and the fear of foreign infiltration do not currently permit a purchase in this province.

But the record producer! Höller interrupts the gnome. Has acquired the castle at a time when more stable conditions prevailed. Today one must be careful and be on guard against becoming the subject of public discussion. While Panella talks, his pupils roll like billiard balls through his eye sockets, and his fingertips drum a steady rhythm on the file folders. Rent what you cannot buy!

Höller nods.

Well, says Panella, I'll meet you tomorrow at four in the piazza. We will visit an appropriate property.

And the financial matters? Höller asks as he rises.

I know your financial situation, Panella interrupts him. We do not want to dwell on trivialities.

ON THE WAY BACK Höller looks in side streets and doorways, because he wants to know whether the boy is following him again. Several times he stops, closes his eyes, and waits for him to ask for money. What if the boy is a lackey for the lawyer? Ridiculous, he thinks immediately. What reason would Panella have to let a ragged boy work for him? But the boy is different from the other children in the place, and Höller remembers that he has always seen him alone and never with the others and that he speaks differently from them; but this difference may mean many things. Perhaps he comes from one of the southern regions, and his parents came to Castelnuovo as farm workers. Maybe he comes from a different country, which explains why his skin is darker than that of the other children ... Höller breaks off and moves on quickly, angered about the fact that he has wasted his time with nonsensical ideas about a boy, instead of focusing on the *Fantasy*.

As he locks the door of his room in the *pension* and hangs his jacket in the closet, Höller notices that his shirt is clinging to his body with sweat. An attack of vertigo forces him to brace himself against the wall with both hands. He stands like this for a while and tries to breathe deeply, which has always been helpful so far. But this time it takes longer for the dizziness to subside, much longer, Höller thinks, and decides to increase the dosage of the painkiller. He takes a shower and lies down on the bed to gather strength, thinks one hour of sleep will be sufficient. His sudden tiredness is probably the result of his conversation with the lawyer. He must not allow himself to interpret every signal from his body; the grace period which the doctors have given him is far from being over.

Later, screaming in the piazza wakes him and he opens the window. In the middle of the square a couple is fighting. Wildly gesticulating, the man yells at the woman, who tries to run away. The man runs after her and grasps her hair. He strikes her in the face a few times. People look out of windows; the owner stands at the entrance to the bar; but no one assists the woman, not even the *carabinieri* who cross the piazza in their blue Alfa. The woman breaks away, stumbling a few steps until she falls. The man stands beside her for a short time, then he spits at her and disappears into a side street.

That a company such as *Bechstein* can collapse, Höller thinks and closes the window. Later, over an espresso, he describes the shameful scene to the professor, who just shrugs his shoulders and says that the people of this place are selfish and ignorant, typical of this country, which continues to decay day by day. It does not surprise him that a woman was beaten on the piazza, that everyone would watch and the idea did not occur to anyone to help the unfortunate woman. The slightest provocation is enough to cause such a scene. This should not surprise Höller, he says; such scenes were part of everyday life at Castelnuovo. The people in this neighbourhood are dangerous to public safety, but when one of them marches to a different drummer, they showed their true character, as the history of the unfortunate family Bastuzzi proved. And although Höller keeps quiet, because he hopes thereby to bring the man to silence, the professor begins to explain. Höller is annoyed that the professor has once again managed to trap him in the parlour. He is also surprised by the fact that the man changes his tone for the story and now speaks as if he was telling an old legend to children.

An idiot called Sereno Bastuzzi lived in a stable. The barn belonged to a formerly inhabited farmhouse. With him lived his father and mother, who were born idiots and peasants. The idiot had an idiosyncratic view of agriculture. The elder Serenos were considered idiots, because they spoke little and were not involved in village life. They attended none of the numerous festivals and went to church only on Easter Sunday. While all the farmers of the surrounding area had joined together in a cooperative, which sold their products in the markets of Siena, the Bastuzzis drove once a week to Arezzo, where they did not earn nearly as much as the members of the cooperative.

Eccentrics. Loners. Idiots, they were ultimately called, individuals who were better to avoid, in order to save oneself trouble. Sereno had not sent them to school; on a farm one could learn all that is necessary for life, they had explained to the Mayor, who had visited the Bastuzzis on their farm in order to enforce compulsory education.

Without success, he had soon departed and had no longer insisted on adherence to the laws.

After Sereno had taken over his parents' farm, he proceeded to put his agricultural ideas into action. Animals and fruit, he claimed, only thrived in a democracy. There is no rational reason why a farmer should have preferential treatment over his sheep, pigs, cows and chickens.

The first innovation was to hold a weekly *farm parliament*, a meeting of all the people and animals that lived on his property. Every Friday evening, he drove all the animals from the stables and pastures to the space between the house and the outbuildings, where he grouped the animals according to parties. Cattle, sheep, pigs and a chicken party were represented in his parliament. He had himself elected as their first president by decree. He then appointed his parents as his deputies.

During the first meeting of the farm parliament, at the request of the pig party, it was decided that the animals should settle in the farmhouse and the vacant places in the farm buildings should be occupied by the Bastuzzis. Immediately after moving into the barn, Sereno's mother began to cluck like a chicken. Not one word passed her lips; if she could not make herself understood with her chicken language, she used her hands for assistance. For a long time she stumbled around the courtyard, scratching with her feet. If strangers strayed into the farm, the postman foreign tourists, or a door-to-door salesman selling agricultural implements, she fled into the barn, clucking excitedly, her scrawny arms flapping.

The father had appointed himself deputy of the pig party

and lay, other than brief moments of clarity, between the old wooden barrels in the wine cellar, grunting and drunk for weeks. All of the work, the sale of the products in Arezzo, was a burden on Sereno. As a born idiot he did not whine, but toiled, because he already lived like an animal. Every Friday during the farm parliament he called for a vote of confidence and never failed. He had established democracy on his farm, was popular with all the parties: something that the corrupt local politicians could only dream about.

But the domestic harmony that prevailed on his property made the neighbours suspicious. It was to be heard more and more frequently that things were not right at the Bastuzzis. Finally it was demanded that someone must establish order at the pig farm, and a *carabiniere* was assigned to explore the situation.

When he rode over to the Bastuzzis' farm on his Vespa, the St. Bernard barked frantically a few times. Along with the leaders of the parliament, Sereno immediately hurried to the property line with the shotgun ready, to challenge the *carabinieri* to put one step on his property. The *carabinieri* thought it was a joke and laughed, but while he was still laughing he took a load of shot in the thigh. Cursing, he hobbled to his Vespa and drove the fastest route back to the dispatch office.

That same day, Sereno Bastuzzi was overpowered in his yard by a police department cadet and the *carabinieri* from the village and locked in the municipal jail, where drunks usually slept off their intoxication.

Sereno was accused of resistance against government authority and the attempted murder of an officer. He was silent to all accusations, merely reiterated monotonously that he wished to be treated according to the laws of his territory.

Before the hearing he was carefully examined by a court psychiatrist and declared certifiably insane. In no time, Sereno Bastuzzi had been transformed from a harmless idiot to a common dangerous psychopath, who disappeared forever behind the walls of a mental institution.

WHEN HÖLLER COMES to the piazza, he immediately sees the black Lancia. Gesualdo is standing beside it. Again he is wearing the greasy leather cap. On the back seat sits the lawyer Panella. After the dwarf has spotted Höller, he pulls the car door open and slams it shut behind him when he sits next to the lawyer.

The Lancia rolls through the narrow streets of the town center and soon reaches the highway. The dwarf increases the pace between the vineyards, cutting corners; the tyres of the Lancia squeal. After a few kilometres they turn into a path on a hill leading between the trees. In the courtyard of a vineyard the car stops and the lawyer gets out with Höller.

Look, Panella says, and points to a tower-like building up the hill. Up there is La Torre, an auxiliary building that belongs to this property, but for some time has been uninhabited.

Then the caretaker is standing beside the lawyer. While Panella talks to him, the caretaker looks down and turns his cap between his hands.

He was on the phone with the owner, says the lawyer, and the latter had asked him to resolve the matter. He would lose no time; he takes charge of the caretaker and orders him to sit in the car next to Gesualdo. Over a bumpy forest road they drive until they are in front of the tower, which attracts Höller immediately.

Mario will show you the house. Look it over carefully. And if you agree, we will sign the lease, which my mother has already prepared.

The caretaker is waiting by the entrance and leads Höller into a dwelling with a kitchenette, pushes open the doors to two rooms, shows him the bathroom and then climbs up a high steep spiral staircase to the tower, where they find a square room with wide windows in every wall.

From here, says the caretaker, you can see the entire town and the vineyards. Even the castle can be made out in the distance. Look out of the west window; on clear days you can see the tower of the Palazzo Pubblico.

Höller and the caretaker go back down to the yard, where Panella is sitting in the Lancia with a briefcase on his lap.

Have you decided? he asks, while Gesualdo starts the engine.

Höller nods, and the lawyer puts a document on the briefcase. Höller scans it and signs immediately.

In the morning you can move to La Torre, Panella says, and puts the contract in his briefcase.

THE BOY IS STANDING beside him on the piazza again when Höller takes his mobile phone from his jacket.

Do you want to telephone, Signor Brendel? Give me the phone, I will dial for you!

Höller slips him a ten Euro note.

Then I will no longer bother you, the boy says with a sly grin and runs into a side alley.

On his second attempt the housemaid picks up. The woman is again speaking in the dialect that has always disgusted him. It is not possible to speak to his wife. She had to leave the villa early in the morning. She is in court or in the lawyers' offices for hours. She does not know the reasons, but lawyers and journalists were also coming into the villa every day ...

Höller breaks off the conversation and considers what the housemaid's sentences could mean. Probably only that the sales negotiations are now in the crucial phase. So it will not be long until the *Russian Deal* is perfect. The buyers' consultants and lawyers will look into the condition of the business. But his lawyer is reliable. No idea about music, but a first-rate legal expert.

Sitting between the workers in the bar, Höller drinks coffee and learns that they are carrying out repair work on the road to Gaiole, and that their union is planning a warning strike because the automatic adjustment of wages to the inflation rate has been suspended. The men cannot agree on whether the strike will force the government to withdraw its decision. Höller orders two bottles of Chianti and he and the workers drink to their victory.

ARE YOU LEAVING the *pension*? The professor beckons Höller to his table with his *Corriere*. He has been told about La Torre and he proposes to visit Höller once he has settled down.

Leaving here is the right decision, he says at the very moment Signora Carmela serves the coffee. This *pension* is the mirror image of Italy; a little smaller, more shabby, perhaps ...

No politics in my house! the landlady demands, and offended, leaves the room.

He, too, would sooner or later move out, shake off this apathy and no longer suck this stupid air into his lungs ... Höller smokes and remembers that the van will soon be coming to carry his luggage and the stereo equipment to La Torre.

I was able to endure the *pension* during the few days when your wife was here. Your wife's walk made me forget quite a lot. And I also observed your wife from the window, when she crossed the piazza … It does not bother you, if I tell you how much I like your wife …

Höller shakes his head, sees that the pale professor suddenly gets flushed cheeks when he thinks of Sophie. There are small beads of sweat on his forehead.

For years, he says later, I have racked my brains exclusively over the prevailing corruption. And then the door opens, and your wife enters the room in a grey travelling suit. You will not believe it, perhaps because of my age, but as soon as I saw your wife I had a huge erection … Am I getting too personal?

Please continue, Höller says and, probably like the professor, imagines Sophie naked. And, he asks, do you grow excited again when you think about my wife?

Your wife has disappeared from the *pension*. We return to the reality in this house.

And your excitement?

It has faded to a lovely memory. Now, reality descends over it in the form of two marrow-transplanting, sanctimonious ladies from Milan. Tea-drinking, wrinkled mourners, before whom the landlady crawls, because they are the sisters of a corrupt politician. Distasteful conditions, from which every reasonable human must perish. Decay, idiocy, and a hypocritical Catholicism were the foundations of this *pension*.

Allegedly an investigation has been initiated against the priest. It will continue after a short break. No one knows the details, but the rumours in town have not stopped. Some think that the priest's drinking habits were reported to the bishop, others suspect that Don Cesare exhausted the funds that were intended for the renovation of the church roof. In any case, if he may say so, all hell has broken loose in the house of God.

A truck stops in front of the *pension*. Two men in overalls carry Höller's luggage outside.

Believe me, says the Professor in parting, I too will leave this *pension*.

WHEN HÖLLER explains to the truck drivers what needs to be loaded and where they will find the things in his room, the men say they had not counted on the fact that he will ride along with them. So the price for the trip must once again be discussed, as it is indeed no longer a pure cargo delivery. And their vehicles are not equipped to transport people.

It is only a few kilometres. Höller interrupts the transparent attempt to jack up the price; he will pay whatever they require. He overlooks the wink and the smile they both use to communicate the fact that they have succeeded in duping him without too much effort. He wants to leave the Piazza as quickly as possible, so he will not attract attention or perhaps be harassed by the impudent boy again. A little later, he sits trapped between the two men in the cab. Suitcases, bags and the packed stereo are in the truck bed. In front of the supermarket at the city limits, Höller asks the driver to stop. He buys food, drinks, and the necessary articles of daily life. The cashier packs everything in boxes and a female apprentice places them on the truck.

He can see the tower from the highway. The sun is reflected in its windows. In a few minutes he will be in his house, Höller thinks, and leans back confidently. And the smell of the men's body odour does not bother him anymore.

On the steep dirt road the truck is bumped around, even though the driver goes no faster than a walking pace. Höller constantly knocks into the men, apologises, but the two just laugh. The passenger opens a can of beer and drinks. When he hands it to the driver, the car runs into one of the countless potholes, and beer sloshes on Höller's trousers. Again, the men laugh, as if it was a good joke.

At their destination the truck driver puts the luggage and the boxes in front of the entrance, saying they would have to leave immediately for an urgent load, because they had lost time at the supermarket. Therefore they could not help bring the things into the house. Again the same twinkle in the eye that he had in front of the *pension*, but it no longer bothers Höller, who is relieved when the two climb into the cab without another word. The truck leaves behind a cloud of dust, and Höller still hears the rattle and roar, even when it had long since disappeared between the vines and trees. Alone at last, he sits down on one of the cardboard boxes and considers how long it will take to drag the things into the house and to find a suitable place for them.

He remembers a sentence from the professor: Your wife's walk made me forget a lot …

Has Don Cesare actually exhausted the church funds?

How are the old men from the farm? The ones he has not seen for several days?

Trifles that he cannot waste his time over! Now that he has found the house, there should be no further delays!

A motorcycle drives up the hill over the bumpy dirt road. As it comes closer he recognizes the caretaker, who shortly thereafter shuts off his engine beside the boxes.

I am bringing you the keys, and so I will help you carry the boxes into the house. Look east! In less than an hour it will rain.

THE GUSTY WIND has grown into a storm that churns the cypress and olive trees. Somewhere in the house a window casement bangs and Höller runs into all of the rooms to close the shutters and windows. In the living room there are still unopened boxes and luggage. So far, all he has done is connect the stereo in the tower, where Höller has placed one table, a chair, and the couch. The boxes are situated so that they form an equilateral triangle with the table. Nothing in the tower should distract him from his preparations.

While he is making coffee in the kitchen and the storm is getting stronger, (even thunder can be heard now), he remembers the fear of hell that he suffered as a child during every storm. And that his father believed he could *drive* that fear away with *shock treatment*.

When he had crept up to his room after the first thunder of an approaching storm, had taken refuge in his bed and had pulled the blanket over his head, his father sought him out in his hiding place and dragged him outside. Hysteria was something for bored ladies, but not for someone who would one day take over his business. His father pushed the boy down the stairwell in front of him, down the hall and out into the fresh air, where the first flashes of lightning already cut through the darkness. He tried to protect his eyes from the glaring light with his hands, but no sooner had he pressed his hands over his eyes, then his father pushed them back down and forced him – do not dare to close your eyes – to consider the terrible lightning images and hear the horrendous noise from the storm and thunder. He ordered the boy to stand motionless in the middle of the garden, and if he moved even one step away from the centre of the garden, threatened him with consequences that he had not forgotten his entire life. Höller did not recall how long he stood in the garden, only the fact that after the *shock treatment* he lay in bed for several days with a severe cold. But this could not shake his father's conviction that the *shock treatment* had been an important step in the development of his personality.

Heavy rain and hail stones beat against the shutters. Höller concentrates on the rhythm of the blows and tries to figure out what piece of music would fit it. Liszt, Mephisto Waltz, perhaps ...

The claps of thunder snatch him from his thoughts. He makes his way to the ground floor, where he discovers a leaky window in the kitchen. He wipes up the puddle below the window with a rag, looking for the place where it needs to be sealed. The rain has pressed wet earth through a gap under the door, caked the floor of the hall. Höller loosens it from the tiles with a bread knife from the kitchen. When he wants to sit up, a sudden dizziness forces him to his knees. The room blurs into an indistinct suggestion. He closes his eyes; he opens them for a brief moment; there is no down and up; then his forehead is on the damp stone floor and a metal vice squeezes his skull. In order to drown out the pain he thinks of the *Fantasy*, but before the first chords have died away, he falls away from the music. What he hears are the heavy thrusts of his breathing and a wheezing sound. Then he is seized by the fear that he will suffocate, will suffocate here on this cold stone floor, even before he has killed the alien in his head and Brendel has played the *Fantasy*.

Later, after he has tried several times without success, he is able to pull himself up on the sink. He finds the pain killers in his pocket. After he has swallowed two of them and leaned against the wall for awhile with his eyes closed, he feels the pressure in his head evaporate, and the images before his eyes tremble a little more faintly.

Höller makes coffee, walks with the cup through the rooms on the ground floor. The most urgent work is done; he will tackle the rest in the morning, when he can see the potential damage in the light of day. His back hurts with every step. And his trousers are caked to the knees with dirt.

The storm has moved off and Höller begins to stow the contents of the cardboard boxes in the crates. In order to prepare himself for the *Fantasy*, he decides to spend the first night in the tower.

Long after midnight, Höller climbs high up to the tower and opens the west window. Damp air moves into the room. Soon he is freezing and slips shivering under the blanket on the couch. Höller recalls the neurologist's advice to spend as much time as possible in the fresh air, because that allegedly reduces the probability of attacks of dizziness. The arrogant brain surgeon also recommended that he pay attention to his diet, and looked at her reflection incessantly in the glass of the picture window while she spoke with the intonation of a priest. The first neurologist at the University Hospital was only interested in the impression he made; Höller no longer interested him. He had checked off the hopeless patient already, once the computer image no longer left any way out. He must have thought that there was nothing to gain with this patient, Höller reasons. An inoperable tumour does not give him the slightest chance of self-recognition; he cannot demonstrate anything with such a patient, cannot even justify the appointment, much less attempt a revolutionary method of operation and then subsequently present it at conferences around the world. Such a patient should not be assigned to him, even if he is a private patient. These cases are for his run-of-the-mill senior physicians, under whose knife they will die one by one anyway ...

When Höller asked what reason he had to care about his diet after the staggering diagnosis, the offended neurological authority was silent, supposing only that the state of time remaining to him depended solely on Höller himself ... The chief physician broke off in the middle of a sentence, probably realised, while he droned his rehearsed formulas to himself like a mantra, the ridiculousness of his advice, and looked at Höller as if he was an enemy who, after it had been established through the course of his disease, had questioned his reputation as a doctor. He probably just thought about the fastest way he could get rid of the inconvenient patient and be on his way to the golf course, where he would forget about the inoperable tumour in a round with the health minister.

In the waiting room, Höller received a card from the secretary on which the date of his next examination was recorded. He threw the card into a waste basket as he left the hospital. Why should he let himself be examined any further? There was no doubt; the diagnosis was final. And he received only vague information from all the doctors regarding the remaining time he had left. An accurate progression is impossible to predict; no case is like another; for this reason it would be important to document the course of the illness, to try and gain knowledge necessary for the treatment of similar cases ... His waiting for the end as part of a field study. Höller would never consider giving permission to be abused as a guinea pig for a series of medical investigations.

Again it starts to rain lightly, and Höller closes the window.

Beneath the covers, he tries to think of the *Fantasy*, closes his eyes and wants to imagine Brendel at the piano; he sees the furrowed brow, the eyes, pupils wide with fright behind thick glasses, his hands resting on his thighs. Höller is waiting for the opening chords, but before Brendel raises his hands over the keys, the picture blurs. No concert hall, no podium with the shiny black grand piano, no tone to be heard in the silence, nothing, merely emptiness, and behind him the wide glass doors of the university clinic open without a break; people walk past him; jostle him; mumble excuses or swear at him; why does he stand in the middle of the way; one is in a hurry; was ill himself or on the way to a close relative who was dying; and he is obstructing their way; robbing them of precious time, so that when one reaches the person who is waiting for them, they may no longer be conscious …

Höller left the spot in front of the hospital entrance and wanted to go to the car park, where he had parked his car. Despite the warnings, he had driven alone in the car. The gliding reassured him; he felt protected from the outside; it was as if there was only him and everything around him was merely a mirage, unreal, like a film.

After a few metres the perplexity: Where should he drive? After the talk with the professor, he did not want to go back to work right away; could also not imagine sitting at a desk and working as if there was not an invincible enemy in his head. He could, as he had sometimes done lately, get into the car and drive off without a destination; insert a CD he had burned a few weeks ago, the slow movements of Schubert's last sonatas; the tones would die away over the whir of the engine; he would glide through the landscape, would notice the light traffic on the roads only in passing, dodge an obstacle from time to time or, because he drove slowly, would be overtaken by a small car with a roaring engine; would pay attention to the differences in the interpretations; hear the worlds that lie between Richter, Leonskaja, and Brendel; the music would dissolve the pressure in his head and, even if not dissolved, then push into the background …

But suddenly, this fatigue among the people outside the hospital. He stood as if paralyzed, while everybody around him was in motion. The pedestrians were dancing bowling pins without faces. Höller closed his eyes, stood a few moments, then went to the park, which insulated the hospital building from the busy main road. A dark brown squirrel crossed his path, ran up a tree trunk and had already disappeared in the leafy crown. On most benches people sat in sleeping bags. He passed them without looking.

Later, he sat down next to a young woman in jeans and a leather jacket, who had nodded absently when he asked whether or not the spot next to her was free. Höller observed her from the corner of his eye; the woman reminded him of his daughter. He knew this distracted look, aimed at a far distant point, from Nathalie. Whenever he confronted her with things which she did not want to face, she looked past him and did not say another word for hours. When she emerged out of her silence, she seemed to have gained strength and hurled accusations at him head on. He could not answer because she did not pause between her sentences, and screamed at him for a long time until, exhausted, she left the area and shut herself in her room. At some point he had realised the futility of his efforts and avoided any serious discussion with Nathalie, whereupon Sophie reproached him: he did not care about his children; his behaviour constitutes the offence of mental cruelty, and he should be happy that they were at home and not in the court-room, because there they would denounce his behaviour, so that the judge would have no choice but to condemn him. A gentle soul like Nathalie was more vulnerable than most people who lack sensitivity, said Sophie, and had avoided him for several days after Höller had pointed out the pathetic absurdity of her complaint. Nathalie was not a *gentle soul* but rather someone *who rejects reality*, someone who hides behind their supposed sensitivity in order to break all the rules because they think only of themselves and, encouraged by Sophie, thinks the world revolves solely around her and her wishes. Which would be understandable; but what made the whole thing impossible was the fact that she herself was not aware of her own needs, which also changed depending upon her moods.

On the bench beside the young woman was a book, and Höller asked if he had disturbed her reading; said she may continue to read; he would not interrupt. Without looking at him, the woman held the book towards him. Just read the title! she whispered, almost soundlessly, as if she wanted to let him in on a secret that should remain hidden from the other visitors in the park. *A Time Without Death* Höller read, and the name of the writer, whom he was sure he had never heard of. Which did not mean anything, because for many years he had read only musicological books and biographies of pianists. Spanish, Portuguese? Höller asked. Portuguese, the woman whispered, but that was not important. The title … What did he expect from such a novel, she asked, and Höller saw that tears were rolling down her cheeks. He was silent. He had no answer to the young woman's question; he looked for an explanation for her tears.

Perhaps there was a man close to her who was dying. Or had

died, and she perceived the novel as a vile mockery of their fate. Hated the author as if he had written his book against them and their lives. Höller, too, knew this about Nathalie: every book, every movie, yes, even political crises always applied to her. She always stood on the losing side, saw the defeat as if it was hers, and forgot about her own life; was powerless and aimless; Sophie however did not want to admit it and therein saw once again evidence for the enormous sensitivity of their daughter. Or wanted to see, because she knew as little about how to deal with their daughter's life as he did, but was not willing to admit this.

What was wrong with the woman? Höller pondered, while she dried her tears and put the book back on the bench, but this time with the back cover facing up, as if she wanted the title to disappear. The author received the Nobel Prize for his work, she said later, without looking at Höller. With a broken voice, as if she was speaking only to herself. And suddenly Höller felt the title to be just as unreasonable as the young woman did. *A Time Without Death* in the hospital park, which was at this time almost exclusively full of patients. Seriously ill, terminally ill, thought Höller. Temporary, like him, who had written off the medicine. But what did that have to do with the woman beside him? She was young. Were it not for the tears and the lost look, she would be a woman that men would follow after.

The novel, she interrupted Höller's reflections, tells of a country where suddenly no one dies. There are no deadly accidents, invalids cease their wasting away, however much they wish for salvation through death, and the aged become as old as the hills and will not die. After a short time the ratios disarrange themselves, because children are born and so the country's population grows rapidly, while it decreases in all other

European countries. Death becomes a luxury item that clever people get through criminal measures, and it becomes an existential problem for the state, which finally joins forces with a criminal organisation in order to eliminate the threat of overpopulation ... Why, she asked after a long pause, while she puts the book in her bag, would someone write such a cynical novel?

Höller was silent and thought about Nathalie. How would she react if she knew how much time he had left? After a few seconds of terror would she talk about alternative methods of healing, even though she knew nothing about it? Would she, with her erratic sentences, none of which agree with each other, lash out against traditional medicine, and know no more at the end of her monologue, for which or against what she was drawn into the fight, to look into the void for a few moments and then lock herself in her room in order *to protect herself from the world*? Höller could not imagine the reaction of his daughter. The most likely would probably be that she took no notice of the diagnosis, like so many things that she did not want to admit ... Höller broke off and asked himself whether or not he had started his deliberations from completely false assumptions. Why did he assume that the diagnosis will upset Nathalie? Perhaps she would react like Clemens and view his death solely from the perspective of the inheritance.

Come! The young woman was standing up. She knew a café she would like to invite him to. He should not consider it intrusive, but this morning she cannot endure being alone. Höller was immediately ready. On the one hand, being with the unknown woman kept him from thinking about whether or not he should go to the meeting with the neurologist; on the other hand, it flattered him that this woman, who could be his daughter, had invited him. Although that was under special circumstances, he had to admit to himself, because probably, if she were not depressed, the woman would not have noticed him. And she certainly would not have spoken of the novel; there was clearly a relationship between it and her depression. As he drove the car on the busy thoroughfare, the woman mentioned a café in the city centre. Höller knew it would take a half-hour or longer and he was surprised by the fact that, in his condition, if only for a moment, he was taken in by his vanity.

The café was one of those traditional taverns that are recommended in every city guide, because one can allegedly recapture the atmosphere of the imperial city and genuine Art Nouveau. A place, therefore, which was mainly visited by tourists and shunned by the locals. Höller had hardly pushed the swinging door open when they encountered the first group of Japanese, friendly smiling people with expensive cameras in front of their chests and ridiculous nylon hats on their heads. A waiter, naturally in a dinner jacket with a black bow tie, tried in abominable English, that those who aspire to sophistication ridiculed with every single word, to direct the group across the room to their reserved seats. In the vicinity of the grand piano Höller discovered an empty table and pulled the young woman by the hand behind him, so they would not lose the place to another guest at the last moment. The cooing Japanese had landed happily in the non-smoking area, but they now sat at a table which separated two Italian families with children of all ages. The Italians were talking over their heads as if they did not exist, and Höller longed for the whisper of the Japanese, because the Italians were talking as loudly as if they were fifty yards away from each other in the Arena of Verona and had to drown out Verdi's "Triumphal March." The children declined the bread; they longed for the usual *panino* and began, after they had given up hope, to destroy the bread on their plates. Soon it would only be good for feeding to the pigeons.

When the waiter finally came to the table, he had to bend in between their heads to be able to take the order over the barrage of Italian words. Since they had taken their seats the woman had not looked at him yet, had not spoken a word, and it suddenly seemed absurd to Höller, to be sitting in a café with a stranger who was obviously completely distraught. Should he ask about the reason for her melancholy? But wouldn't that continue to bother his companion? There he sat in the noise of the café between good-humoured people, and thought about the despair of a stranger, while the deadly tumour lies waiting in his head.

The children at the other tables had their mobile phones in the hands now and played their stored ringtones for each other. The adults did not think that they should stop the non-sense, merely increased their volume to drown out the mobile melodies. They put the telephones away only when a greasy violinist stepped up to the grand piano with an aging matron. After a few strokes of the bow the violin was tuned, and the two played Viennese waltzes. After a few bars, the first Japanese appeared with their digital cameras and a frenzy of flash-bulbs descended on the bored musicians. An Italian sang along with the melody and was not silenced by the scathing look from the waiter.

The young woman looked at him, and Höller discovered tears in her eyes, while the bliss of the waltz cut through the room and encouraged the Japanese to offer a hurricane of applause after the end of the first piece. The violinist took a bow; a lock of gelled hair fell over his eyes, while his companion did not even look up and broke the beginning chords of the next piece into a shimmering glissando, to which the violinist, with a smug smile, tucked his instrument under his chin and began the *Hungarian Dances*. Brahms between *sachertortes* and milky coffee for hordes of swine-eared tourists, Höller thought. But at least no Schubert. Should the two clownish figures get around to Schubert, he decided, he would leave the café. Regardless of whether the woman follows or remains seated. He will not participate in the execution of *his* Schubert ... While the violinist fiddled through the *Puszta* and regaled the yellowing court councillors' widows in the window seat next to the grand piano with his pandering glances, one of the Italian children recognized the melody, pressed a few buttons on his mobile phone and held it up. Seconds later, the *Hungarian Dances* sounded as a polyphonic ringtone from the phone. The ladies in the window seat looked as if they had come into the café directly from the Imperial Crypt. In a black painted hackney carriage, Höller imagined, and heard them sound off against the appalling conduct of today's youth in perfect, *Schönbrunner* German. One of the disastrous consequences of egalitarianism, whispered one, there is no respect anymore, because there are no distinctions ... Because there is no longer a civil society, her friend seconded and rolled her eyes, while the children at the next table could no longer be stopped and their mobile phones were scouring out ever new sounds that they played simultaneously, and the café filled with a cacophonous cloud of sound, which caused the musicians to break off in the middle of the *Puszta*. They would take a short break, whispered the violinist, but his anger at the noise of the children disappeared. *I ragazzi d' oggi sanno usare la tecnica*, Höller heard from their parents' table. The same naive pride, thought Höller, with which Sophie watched their daughter's craziness. Finally, the liberating *Andiamo*, and like a Campanian herd of buffalo, the Italians stormed outside through the narrow aisles between the tables.

Finally! Höller said, but the young woman did not respond. She looked at him and said nothing. All of a sudden he felt superfluous; the childish pride after she had spoken to him and suggested the café gave way to a crippling embarrassment. She needed assistance, that much was certain; but he did not know how he could help another person. Not people and not their troubles. Because it was clear to him that the young woman was in trouble.

Höller ordered two brandies, but although he had asked the woman if she would also like one, he had been sure she would not decline any proposal. She would have nodded wordlessly at any beverage. And then he reminded himself of his father who, every time he complained about something, told him a story that he supposed would *eclipse his lament*. He was always silent after these stories, although as a child he had already suspected that his father's stories were fictional and not, as he had always stressed, *taken from real life*. A story would break the silence, which was still bleak after the Italians had left the cafe. Höller did not want to talk about himself, so, like his father, he had to invent a story. The simplest would be to report on the follies of his daughter, but this would probably hardly help the young woman's depression. So while he smoked a cigarette and emptied the cognac glass, he invented a pianist who for many long years lived in his grand piano, which he left only for absolute emergencies and reluctantly. One day, however, this pianist had climbed out of the piano, had slammed the lid on the strings and locked the keyboard. Then he drove to the lake at the outskirts of town and stared at the gossamer undulations of the waves there a while with the key in his hand …

The young woman looked up from her glass, and Höller saw how her despair began to give way to bemusement. If this continued, he reflected, the crucial step would be taken to save the situation. For this reason he continued to recount it rapidly, because he did not want to risk being interrupted by the woman during a short pause.

The pianist stands at the edge of the lake with the key in his hand, still undecided for a few moments, then he throws the key into the water with his eyes closed. He keeps his eyelids pressed together and waits like that for a long time, until he is sure the lake will no longer reveal the spot where the key sank.

The woman was still listening to him, Höller saw, and he continued. Before the piano player crawled into the grand piano, he had sat for years at the keys, cheered on by a poign-ant teacher with slender hands, for whom nothing existed except the notes. For years he looks back and forth between his hands and notebooks, runs through the city with the sound of music in his head and sits down, still out of breath and fuming from exertion, playing, practising like a madman. He practises so long tendonitis forces him from the piano bench. Then he lies under the grand piano and hears sounds, as if the teacher was playing. The pain in his wrists burns up through his arms, soon reaching his head and destroying the sounds, until later the dead silence prevails in his head. And in this dead silence he imagines the slender hands of the teacher, the mazurkas dancing … Finally, he crawls out from under the grand piano because he cannot see enough of these slender hands, and finally he rescues himself from under the grand piano and runs to his doctor, where he cowered in between sweaty patients waiting until he was called into the examination room. But none of the so-called experts understands his plight. He says: With each day of treatment, the sounds continue to withdraw further from him. The specialists immediately look away. Before the doctor, who is to cure him of the inflammation, flips through his box of index cards and waits until the pianist has left the room, a final attempt to explain: Each day of inflammation increases the reduction of pressure in his head, the sounds first diminish and later, they are exhausted, devoured ... Helpless experts; from time to time an anxious glance behind protective glasses; a drug name, usually beginning with *Dolo*, scratched on a form; a dismissive shake of the hand, which again causes pain in his wrists, and he is on the road. Left with the decision, whether or not he should seek medical attention or creep back under his grand piano. The same game is repeated at ever shorter intervals. The pianist practises in order to encounter the teacher's sound; runs to the doctor; hunches down under the grand piano; practises; always the same game. Each piece writes its own history of pain into his bones and sinews, until one of the doctors talks about *depletion*, of *permanent damage*, describes his crippling existence to him and sends him out of the consulting room with the sentence: Forget the piano ... But how can he forget the piano when his head is filled with ballads and sonatas and impromptus and nocturnes? If an excess pressure of sound prevails in his head, can't it escape through a valve?

In a book, he reads about a man who runs through the city carrying a head that contains an excess pressure of sound similar to his own. Time and again, this man runs to the bridge through narrow streets enclosed by high houses, until one day he throws his head into the water. But the pianist's own head is still attached; he could only do it by throwing his body off the bridge. But that, he knows, did not work out for Schumann: no relief, just a devastating pneumonia … With folded arms, the pianist encircles the grand piano, he wraps his burning head, in which there is a heavy pressure of sound, with cooling cloth that he has to change every few minutes. Eventually, he opens the lid over the strings and climbs into the grand piano. He *thrusts* his head into the hammers, and after a short time he feels the pressure in his head give way. He rises from the instrument; his head begins to fill with sound again. If he returns to his grand piano, the pressure drops immediately. So the pianist leaves the grand piano only in the most necessary cases, is completely free from pain, apart from a few inconsequential knots in the muscles of his back.

Although Höller knew he had finished his story without a real conclusion, he walked past the musicians, who again performed the Viennese waltz, to the toilet, where he remained for some time and hoped the young woman would have calmed down a bit. But when he returned to the table, he saw that his companion had left the café.

GESUALDO drums against the door with his fists. Höller opens.

Come! cries the dwarf, and is already sitting in the black Lancia. The *Avvocato* sends me. It is court day on the piazza. They need your testimony.

But I'm still in my underwear. I need time to put something on.

We have no time!

On the piazza the Lancia drives through the crowd, which recedes slowly. In the centre of the square there are tables and chairs. *Carabinieri* and ushers are to be seen. When Höller steps out of the car in his underwear, the crowd hoots.

Approach! he hears Panella's voice.

Slowly Höller goes toward the tables, where he discovers the *Avvocato* in a black robe with a red collar. Beside him sits his mother. When she sees Höller, she begins to laugh and shouts over and over: What a pathetic figure, what a pathetic …

Suddenly an eerie peace prevails over the piazza. Sit! Panella orders, and a *carabiniere* shoves a chair behind Höller and pushes him down. We are trying a case against your wife, who is accused …

Gesualdo drums against the door with his fists.

Höller opens. Ends up half-dressed on the square in front of the judge's table. The same *carabiniere* pushes him into the chair.

We are negotiating against your wife, who is accused …

Gesualdo drums against the front door.

Piazza.

Carabiniere.

Chair.

We are negotiating today …

Bathed in sweat, Höller is startled from his nightmare and goes down to the ground floor, where he stands for a long time under the hot shower. Later, he drinks coffee and climbs up to the tower, which is filled with the morning sun. The silver controls of the stereo flash.

Brendel plays Schubert's *B flat Sonata*.

During the second movement, Höller looks out of the window and recognises the farm on the opposite hilltop. The old men and the violent administrator cross his mind. In the south, he sees Castelnuovo with its tightly packed houses. Of the castle, where the Mayor has his work space, only the roof can be made out. In the west, hills and as a vague suggestion in the morning mist, Siena. In the north, woods, endless vineyards, now and then a farmhouse.

The storm has devastated the area in front of the house. There is water in the deep potholes. Everywhere rubble and broken branches. A barrel has rolled down the slope and has burst against a concrete pillar. Once Brendel has played the Sonata to the end, he will go outside and clear away the traces of the storm.

For a while, Höller stands in the open doorway and looks over the front garden. Wet earthworks, standing water where birds cavort. The storm has broken stones from the boundary wall and washed them out of place, as if they were made of cardboard. Up close the devastation is greater than he assumed after the view from the tower window. He thinks of the *Fantasy* and the fact that he must not lose any time; he does not want to put the performance at risk. The response from England has not yet arrived, but he has to continue his planning as though he had Brendel's commitment. And Höller has no doubt that he will obtain it. But La Torre is now the headquarters for the *Fantasy* project; journalists will soon be arriving. They would see the miserable condition of the property after the storm; they would doubt that a definitive interpretation can be organised from here, and lose their interest after the first visit.

Höller considers where he will begin his work, and decides to set the first stones of the retaining wall in place, because this requires the greatest strength. The doctor's warning to avoid physical exertion, because that could trigger a crisis, he ignored. What does the word *crisis* mean in his circumstances?

Only that he must increase the dosage of the painkiller one more time. Now it is about the *Fantasy* and not the doctor's discomfort.

Höller crosses the square; after a few steps, heavy clods of earth stick to his soles and the leather on the top of his shoes is damp. When he tries to lift the first stone, he realises that he lacks the strength. Beside the barn, he finds an iron bar. With its assistance, he succeeds in rolling the stone to the property's boundary. After he has completed removing all of the bricks from the area Höller sits, out of breath, on the boundary wall. His shirt sticks to his body, his palms burn, and his back hurts. He tries to remember the last time he worked with his hands. Despite the exhaustion, he is relieved. He has completed the most difficult part of the work and sees this as a positive sign: the *Fantasy* will live to see its ultimate interpretation in Castelnuovo.

Höller imagines the reconstructed community hall, sees Brendel coming into the hall hours before the concert. Plaid jacket; corduroy trousers; the surprised look behind the thick glasses; a few more steps to the grand piano …

Suddenly, a gentle bump against his forearm. Beside him sits a tri-coloured cat. The head above the amber-coloured eyes is white, as well as the chest and belly, while the back and tail are varying shades of gray-brown shining in the sunlight. She does not flinch when he strokes her on the head. Höller goes into the kitchen, finds sausage leftovers in the refrigerator. When he comes out of the house, the cat is sitting next to the front door. She eats the pieces of sausage from his hand. Later, while he collects twigs and broken branches and stacks them against the outer wall of the barn, he observes the animal, always a few steps behind him. And when he walks down the slope to collect the broken barrel staves, the cat follows him.

In the house, Höller notes that his shoes are hopelessly ruined and throws them into the rubbish bin. His trousers are caked with dirt up to the knees, but they will have to be salvaged. He pours himself a brandy and again tries to remember the last time he worked with his hands, but nothing comes to mind.

He stands under the shower for a long time; the warm water running over his skin feels pleasant and he feels the weariness leaving his body. In the tower, he listens again to the *B flat Sonata* and looks out the window. The cat runs around the barn; she has probably picked up the tracks of some prey. Höller is caught by her lithe movements; compulsively he follows her path and waits when she disappears out of his sight for a short time, intent on the fact that she will emerge again. In these moments, he feels something like confidence; nothing will get in the way of the *Fantasy* ...

IN THE EARLY AFTERNOON, without Höller having noticed his coming, the caretaker stands in the entrance hall. He says he wanted to see what damage the storm had caused. Höller talks about his work, glad to have a common interest with the man.

That would not have been necessary, says the caretaker, I would have sent workers. In an hour, all the damage would have been removed. Certainly the *Avvocato* would not think it was right that you must carry out the work that should be completed by the owner. You will nevertheless report it to him?

Höller calms the caretaker, says it had made him happy to work for himself again. After they have drunk brandy, they go to the front garden.

The road that leads up the hill is in a terrible state, Höller says. Potholes, gravel, rubble. A cart path. When my preparations for the ultimate performance of the *Fantasy* are completed, visitors from all over the world will come to La Torre in their luxury cars. Music experts and arts administrators. They would not expect such a road.

The caretaker shrugs his shoulders regretfully, says his workers also curse about the road. Time and again barrels full of grapes fell off the bed of the tractor trailer, but the complaints about the road did not interest the owner in Milan. He only cared about the accounts. The profits meet his satisfaction; he is going back to Milan and will only return in a year, when the next payroll is due. And then the caretaker is silent for some time, but Höller sees that he is thinking hard, looking into the distance, and how he self-consciously beats his cap against his thigh. Barely audible, he later says, your musicians and your fantasies will be unimportant to the *Cavaliere*. He is only interested in his race horses and their prize money.

And while the caretaker finishes describing a Milanese snob, Höller imagines the chief critic of the *Neue Zürcher*, after hours of driving over mountain passes and highways, turning into the gravel path at the *foot* of the hill. Eyes burning with fatigue behind rimless glasses, unable to avoid the deep potholes. Stones as big as fists are hurled against the undercarriage by the wheels. "Surprise Symphony," he will think after the first blow and bump his head against the windshield. The lenses of his glasses cracked. Blood dripping on his silk shirt. Until he reaches La Torre. He is a cripple …

I'll take care of the condition of the road, Höller says, while the caretaker is still talking about a horse race in Paris. Shortly before the owner's horse reaches the goal, the narration breaks off.

You are only the tenant, you can not …

Talk to the owner, Höller interrupts him. If I cover the cost of asphalting and waive any claim, he will agree.

Consider the costs! the caretaker says.

This is about the *Fantasy*. Talk to the owner!

Only now does Höller notice that the caretaker is speaking to him slowly, while he answered the *Avvocato* or Gesualdo at such a tempo that Höller understood only individual words. *Allegro con fuoco*, thinks Höller, in contrast to the difficult *Adagio*, which he keeps in readiness for him. But that's probably because the caretaker speaks with his fellow countrymen in dialect, while in discussion with him he tries to use standard language. And the man is to be praised for this effort; he inserts pauses again and again, searching for a word or pronunciation, sometimes merely to correct an emphasis.

Höller knows that the caretaker connects nothing with the word *fantasy* and cannot explain to himself why, because of a single word, a road should be paved. As long as he can remember, he has worked with his hands, worked hard, until he succeeded in becoming the caretaker of the estate. And that was because he has worked more than others, harder and longer, without complaining or striking with the trade unions if late at night those labourers left and there was no end in sight. He has become the caretaker, the man will think, because he lives in the real world, where there is no room for the *Fantasy*. That is something for the rich and powerful, for the *cavalieri* or the Mayor. It would also be something for the *Avvocato*, but Panella is too intelligent to waste his time with fantasies.

The caretaker leaves Höller standing in the middle of the square and goes to the boundary wall, checking its condition by pressing with his boot sole against stones. Then he disappears for a short time into the barn. He probably hopes that after his return Höller would no longer talk about the road. And no more about the *Fantasy*, which he cannot picture.

But look at you! Your trousers are ruined! the caretaker exclaims and jerks Höller from his thoughts. Only now does he realise that after his shower, he slipped back into the same trousers, which he wore while working in the front garden this morning.

That's nothing, Höller says. He would take the trousers to the cleaner's later. There is just one dry cleaner in Castelnuovo?

Yes, the caretaker says, and the corner of his mouth twitches. He looks around for help. Do not take the trousers to the cleaner's. If the condition of your trousers reaches the *Avvocato*'s ears, he will reproach me; perhaps he will even notify the owner in Milan. And this could result in sudden anger towards him … Do not take your trousers to that place! Come into the caretaker's house. My wife shall clean and press your trousers. She will also repair the inside seam.

Fine, Höller says, but in return you will speak to the owner about the road.

The caretaker nods and starts his motorbike.

Saddle up!

Höller clings to the man with both arms and sees obstacles and potholes hurdling towards them. Take it slow! he cries, but the caretaker does not hear him. The man moves, Höller thinks, the same way he speaks in dialect. *Allegro con fuoco.* And the rattling of the exhaust introduces a gruff *basso continuo* under the melody of the engine. When a van comes towards them at a narrowing of the road, Höller closes his eyes and presses his head against the caretaker's shoulder. Only when he turns off the engine in the courtyard of the estate, does Höller sit up again. With trembling knees, he follows the man into the house.

THE CARETAKER'S WIFE looks at the trousers and shakes her head. She asks if Höller fell off. Circuitously, her husband tells her about the clean-up work and now avoids the use of dialect in his house, which obviously unsettles his wife. Höller stands in the middle of the room. The caretaker's wife walks around him a couple of times, touches the trouser fabric and says they must be washed. Give me your trouser, Signor Brendel!

Höller hesitates, thinks of the absurdity if he faces the two in his underwear, and remembers Sophie's answer when he asked where her confidence in the court room came from and how she always managed not to get upset, even when the proceedings seemed to progress to her disadvantage. She imagines her opponents in their underwear: the judge, the prosecutor, the jurors, the whole senile, varicose-veined squadron, and she knows that she cannot lose against these caricatures.

The caretaker's wife leaves the room and soon returns with a pair of black trousers, which she hands to Höller and asks him to step into them carefully. These are the trousers that go with her husband's Sunday suit, which he also wears when the owners come for the annual payment.

How long will it take? Höller asks the caretaker and puts on the trousers, which are too wide and too short for him. Only a small improvement compared to the image he would have rendered in his underwear, Höller thinks. When he stands upright, he must hold the waistband with one hand.

Two hours, maybe a little longer, the woman says and supposes, before leaving the room with them over her arm, he would at least stay for dinner; then he could return to La Torre in his own trousers.

The caretaker, who had been looking out of the window self-consciously for some time, says he still has some work to do in the wine cellar. He carries a jug of red wine and some crumpled magazines. In order to drive away the boredom, he whispers, and the Chianti is excellent; he had obtained a good price at the trade fair in Verona.

For a while Höller looks out of the window and observes the workers who are dragging the feed and fertilizer sacks into a warehouse. Later, he leafs through a magazine that is more than a year old. He reads the story of a nonagenarian who married his childhood friend, an octogenarian, after they had lost sight of one another for a lifetime. The journalist used an entire paragraph to describe the tone of voice in which they promised each other never to leave. Perhaps, Höller reasons, while I read this sentimental story, both of them are long dead …

A look at his wristwatch: Not a half hour has passed since the wife left the room with his trousers. Höller goes outside, one hand on the waistband. On a line behind the caretaker's house, he finds a clothespin, pulls the waistband together at the back and clamps it tight. After a few cautious steps, he notes, the caretaker's trousers are seated firmly on his hips.

At dinner he is offered the caretaker's place at the front end of the long table, where the children and farmhands also sit. While waiting for the food, the young children stare openly at him; the adults examine Höller from the corners of their eyes. Before they begin to eat, one of the caretaker's sons says grace. Not a single word is said, but even while they shove enormous rolls of pasta into their mouths and noisily chew, the men observe him.

After a glass of wine, which even the smallest children drink, the caretaker sends the workers outside with new instructions. Höller praises the pasta and asks casually about his trousers. She has already taken them out of the dryer and hung them on the line, the wife says; soon he could put them back on.

Höller continues to sit at the table with the caretaker's children. They lay out their school books and begin their homework.

And how did you like the stew? one of the girls asks without looking at him.

Excellent!

Excellent, the child repeats, even though it was a cat?

Höller is silent; he does not know what the girl expects from him.

It was a feral cat that our tomcat tore apart and left outside the door. With horrible bite wounds in its neck, the girl says. The cat was on the stone steps outside the doorway. And our tomcat guarded it. A long time, until mother carried it into the kitchen. You actually tasted the stew?

Your trousers! The caretaker's wife stands in the doorway with Höller's trousers and sends the children out of the room so he can change clothes. You must eat regularly, she says when he has taken off the caretaker's trousers. Your legs are too thin …

When he offers her money for the work she stretches out both hands to him defensively. Outside the entrance to the wine cellar he meets the caretaker, who brings him back to La Torre on his motorbike. The owner agrees to pave the road with asphalt, he shouts to him during the journey, and reminds

Höller of his promise to tell the lawyer Panella nothing about the dirty trousers.

Finally back in the tower. A lost afternoon. Hours wasted in the caretaker's house and not the slightest progress. In order to prepare for the work, Höller listens to the *Fantasy*. With closed eyes he lies on the couch and imagines Brendel at the piano. In the *Adagio*, he feels like the music comes to rest again in him. With each measure he grows calmer, sees his goal clearly in front of him and considers the next steps.

The paving of the road needs to be addressed. Höller remembers the construction crew workers in the bar who talked about an imminent warning strike. The men do repair work on the road through to Gaiole. He will be able to come to an agreement with them, since they will certainly be interested in a supplement to their starvation wages.

If the road is improved, a meeting with the old men from the farm must be arranged, because Höller intends to hire them as ushers. He will not consider Gesualdo, who plays an obscure role in the place. His dependence on the Mayor and Panella is obvious, but not the reasons that drove him to it. The professor's insinuations come to mind. The prison in Volterra. Perhaps Gesualdo is a convicted murderer? And a man with blood on his hands is unthinkable as an usher. He will book the old men as ushers. They are without work and definitely feel useless most of the time. And that is why they will have the greatest enthusiasm in the matter.

Brendel flies through the *allegro* of the last movement, and Höller has also arrived at the conclusion of his deliberations. He stands at the open window and looks at the roof of the palace, where at this time the Mayor is probably sitting at his desk and still has no idea that he will tear down and rebuild the community hall. As a concert hall, perfect in the smallest detail … A perfection, Höller thinks, which is not even found in cities.

His visit to the castle must be prepared. Everything depends on it. If he is convincing, if the intonation and the rhythm of his sentences are correct, the Mayor will not oppose his plans. For that reason alone, not because the plans will make his sleepy farming village a musical metropolis. A point on the map that every music expert will know after the ultimate performance of the *Fantasy* …

The biggest problem is to engage with the Mayor. Höller has only once seen the man in the village hall and has heard his voice for only a few sentences. Moreover, he cannot estimate the impact of this exceptional situation. How much had the presence of the politicians influenced the man? Is his tone different when he sits at his desk and makes decisions? Is he an enemy of music?

Höller listens to the *Fantasy* again.

WHEN HÖLLER looks from the tower window the next morning, he sees the tri-colored cat stretching in the sun in the centre of the courtyard. For a while he watches the animal, and believes that the cat detected him long ago and is waiting for him to drop a couple of pieces of leftover sausage. The presence of the cat calms Höller. He will make up for the short delay caused by the storm by focusing with renewed confidence on the *Fantasy*. Against all the doctor's advice, he has worn himself out, worked to exhaustion, and the headaches have not increased. Only his back and his palms ache, and his arm muscles, but that happened to anybody who is not accustomed to manual labour. He did not increase the dose any further this morning and feels the pain only as a vague indication from afar, like something that has nothing to do with him, Höller thinks.

In the refrigerator, he finds remnants of sausage and a little cheese. He cuts both into small bites and carries them outside on a plate. Now the cat runs up to him and eats without looking up once. When she has licked the plate clean with her long tongue she begins to clean her head, by first moistening one of her paws and then drawing it with frantic movements across her face. Later, Höller is sitting on the doorstep; she comes closer and rubs her head against his leg, lets herself be stroked across the back and purrs so loudly that she drowns out the birds in the pines. From now on, he will make sure that there is always something in the house for the cat.

While he observes how the cat stretches beside him in the sun and finally rolls into a ball of fur to sleep, he remembers Sophie's aversion to pets. They only distract their owners from their duties and responsibilities and cause damage to the house. And if not damage, they would get everything dirty and bring in germs. Nathalie had managed for several days to hide a small cat from Sophie, who spent most of the time at home studying case files and investigation logs. When she accidentally found animal hair on Nathalie's blanket, however, she insisted that she take the kitten away from the house on the same day. Therefore, for several days, Nathalie could not go to school and did not speak a word.

Sophie's disgust with animal hair reminds Höller of Glenn Gould's hypochondria, whose Bach interpretations he had heard again and again, before he began to throw himself exclusively at Brendel; that exclusivity did not allow him to concentrate on anything else. What had impressed him above all was the anarchy that Gould applied to the tempos of the Brahms ballads, this provocative slowness, which shifted between individual tones to a nervous tension which he had not been able to get enough of for many years. Now, in the tower, Höller recalls the clarity of Gould's fingerings while he observes the sleeping cat at his side from the corner of his eye. And the trills typical of his playing.

Sometimes he practices with a vacuum cleaner running, Gould said, because he can hear the skeleton of the music in this way. He would no longer play the piano when he was fifty, Gould said several times, and died of a heart attack ten days after his fiftieth birthday. The hypochondriac had meant business. One stroke, *a heart attack*, Höller thinks, swept away all doubts and fears; no longer afraid to catch a cold; no longer afraid of hurting his hands … Gould was not married. He had no children, and Höller did not know what he thought about women.

For a long time, Höller looks into the emptiness; he places a palm on the back of the cat, which uniformly rises and falls. A kind of peacefulness emanates from the animal. Once he had read that cats would lower the blood pressure of any man who held one in his arms. But now that has no meaning for him; it is as meaningless as the well-intentioned advice of his doctors. What counts is the *Fantasy*. And the peace that flows from the cat into his body will help him clear all obstacles from the path to his definitive interpretation.

HÖLLER TAKES THE DESOLATE cart path downhill. He has never taken the path to the caretaker's house on foot and he does not know how long he will need. He feels every bump through his thin leather soles, and walking is a torture. He can no longer see the property between the trees and he now walks slowly, in order to avoid the larger stones and holes. In the past, when he wanted to look for a solution to a difficult problem without being disturbed, he had sometimes left his office and walked through the city park. In walking steadily between the trees and bushes, his head was free for new ideas which he had never encountered at his desk. He had been convinced of this; but now he is no longer able to think clearly. He wants to think about the Fantasy, about the next steps, about the English letter (as the clerk at the post office calls it), the crucial meeting with the Mayor. And he cannot even manage the obvious: he does not hear the *Fantasy* while he is stepping over the stones or dodging the water-filled potholes. His walking has no rhythm; in ridiculous syncopation he stumbles to the caretaker's house. Instead of the *Fantasy*, he thinks about the owner in Milan, to whom art is all the same. What an idiot, Höller thinks; he does not know how to do anything better with all his money than to put it on the racehorses. If he would support the *Fantasy*, it would be easy to overcome all the difficulties in the shortest time. For that noble countryman and employer the authorities would bend any law, and if necessary break it, until it corresponded to his wishes. But the snob is interested at most in sentimental bar music, which he uses as an accompaniment to his advances on women who could be his granddaughters.

It has taken more than half an hour until Höller is standing with wet shoes and aching limbs in front of the caretaker's house. There is no one to be seen, and in addition to exhaustion comes confusion. Höller had hoped that the caretaker would drive him into town on his motorbike. He needs to go to the post office; perhaps Brendel's letter has been lying there for days and back in England the pianist is angry because he has not received a reply to his commitment.

My husband is not here! The caretaker's wife is standing in the doorway. Her husband is with the workers, but she does not know where they are employed. The woman speaks slowly, trying to avoid words in dialect; which is more successful for her than for her husband. Would you like coffee? She interrupts Höller's helpless silence and goes inside.

Höller is afraid of losing time again, but follows the woman in order not to offend her. He also hopes that while he drinks his coffee, the caretaker will come back and drive him to Castelnuovo.

After the woman has placed two cups on the table, she takes off her apron and smoothes down the hair on her neck. When Höller smokes, the woman asks him for a cigarette.

She had stopped smoking many years ago, but now she would like to try a cigarette again. After the first puff, she coughs and looks self-consciously out of the window. Höller thinks he should say something now; thank the woman for the invitation; praise her coffee; the order that prevails in her home; perhaps ask about the children; but every sentence that he can think of is ridiculous, and he is silent.

Then, they put out their cigarettes; after she has apologised for her curiosity, the woman asks what she can expect to hear when she listens to the *Fantasy*. Her husband had only supposed that Höller needed the peace and seclusion of La Torre, to be able to concentrate on the *Fantasy*. But the tone in which her husband had spoken was not his own, and she knew immediately that, like her, he too did not know what to expect from the *Fantasy*.

Höller does not know how he should begin, in order to ensure that the woman understands him; he also doubts that she would understand it at all; he tells her about Schubert and his unfortunate life, because he hopes the woman would know what to make of the adversity and the rejection, the *human misery*, Höller says, and is relieved to see that the woman understands him. Then he describes *Schubert's character* and *Schubert's appearance* to her: the thick glasses; the open-air dance festivals and the young girls, the ones *Schubert's eyes cling to*; and, barely audible, sighs from the caretaker's wife, who now sets the silver espresso machine on the gas flame a second time. She waits at the stove until the coffee rises hissing and steaming into the upper container; then she refills the cups and looks expectantly at Höller, whose mind has lost track of the *Fantasy* long ago and is now entangled in a sentimental biography of the artist. When he starts talking about the importance of Schubert's music, Höller sees that the caretaker's wife loses interest. She must now take care of lunch, she interrupts him, and the disappointment over the progress of his story can be seen in her face. The food must be on the table when her husband and the workers came; work delays were not allowed this time of year.

Relieved, Höller breaks off and says he must go to the post office.

But not in those shoes! the woman exclaims. You cannot go into town with those shoes! She will lend him her husband's Sunday shoes and clean and dry his drenched ones. He could then pick them up on his return.

The caretaker's shoes pinch but Höller keeps them on, because he does not want to disappoint the woman and risk further delay. Her husband is using the motorcycle, but he could take her bicycle for the trip to town.

The seat has been adjusted for the woman's height, so Höller must turn his bent knee outward in order to pedal. He rides downhill and avoids the potholes as much as possible. Just before the intersection with the road, he notices that the brakes do not work. There are trees along the path. If he bangs into them, he would not get away without injury, Höller thinks. He also thinks about broken bones and plaster casts, and the fact that in this case he would not be able to work on the *Fantasy* for several weeks. Just before he reaches the road to Castelnuovo, he closes his eyes. He takes it as a positive sign that as far as the eye can see there is no vehicle on the road.

SIGNOR BRENDEL, WHERE are you going? the boy calls after him when he crosses the piazza on the bicycle. Höller does not answer and decides that he will no longer tolerate the boy's impositions. Before he is able to make a plan, he notices that the nuisance is running after him.

Signor Brendel! he calls a few times. Wait! The English letter has arrived!

Höller wants to stop but the brakes do not work again and he drags the caretaker's Sunday shoes over the cobblestones. When he gets off the bicycle and the boy is standing in front of him out of breath and does not utter a word, he sees that there is a deep scar running through the upper leather of a shoe.

The English letter! the boy repeats and seizes the handlebars. I will watch your bike while you are at the post office.

Höller knows that he cannot shake the boy off, and leaves him with the bike. Like a ghost he appears; perhaps the *Avvocato* pays him, in order to know about his every move. Silently they cross the Piazza; the boy pushes the bicycle, while Höller wastes no more thoughts over him and thinks only about the message. Hardly has he entered the room when the postman stumbles into him with it. Höller quickly pushes a fifty-euro note at the man and on the way out sees his disappointment that he does not immediately open the letter. The boy is standing next to the entrance with the bike and watches him with narrowed eyes as he opens the letter. And certainly the disappointment did not escape the small monster when he sees that the letter is not from Brendel, but from Clemens.

He scans it without interest, although he would have preferred to crumple it up after the *Dear Father*, which he has hated for years. The career-chasing snob writes to him from his English study and thinks only about how he could earn money from the *Russian Deal*. Höller is surprised by the fact that he uses the same words as Sophie, and is now certain that she has formed an alliance with the son against him. But this English rat, Höller thinks, wants to protect himself if he should sell the business against Sophie's will, and at least earn something from the sale. In his letter, peppered with empty legal phrases, Clemens offers to lead the negotiations, praising his knowledge in matters of commercial law and his excellent language skills, and concludes that he envisaged ten percent of the selling price as his fee.

After he slipped the boy a Euro, he disappears into a side street without asking any questions or offering his services. Höller pushes the bike over the piazza; he crumples up the wrong English letter in his free hand and later throws it into a waste basket. As he moves along, he reflects that he could not say whether he is more repelled by the meddlesome boy or his own son. Both of them are repulsive, he determines when he mounts the bike at the end of the piazza. Greedy and presumptuous, each in his own way. And something connects the two: at school Clemens had no friends, but had only known competitors who he tried at any price and by all means to leave behind him. He had repeatedly invited colleagues to the villa, presenting them as *friends*, but Höller knew that these invitations only served to impress the invitees or to let him spy on their schemes in a relaxed atmosphere. And he has never seen the irritating boy with other children. They played in the piazza or in the park behind the castle; the boy always held himself apart; was never part of these games; only the observer, who spied on everything from a safe distance; nothing escaped him. And one more commonality between the two, notes Höller: neither of them seems to suffer from his role as an outsider, on the contrary, it seems that they enjoy it and look down arrogantly on all the others.

FOR MORE THAN a quarter of an hour Höller rides on the slightly sloping road to Gaiole, when, without warning, the pressure in his head begins to swell and the images before his eyes blur the way they do on particularly hot days. He must get off the bicycle and sit down on a mile marker beside the road. He thinks about the physicians' warnings to avoid exertion and swallows a pain pill. He feels his pulse throb furiously in the carotid artery and waits with his eyes closed until the pressure subsides and he is breathing evenly again. He then continues his journey and takes care to pedal only so hard that he will not lose his breath a second time. After some time, he discovers the road workers' site office behind a curve in the dense forest.

After Höller has told the foreman his plan they go into the site office, where they sit down at a table with half-full beer bottles and the remnants of a snack. Technically, the reconstruction of the road on the hill is no problem, says the foreman, but he does not think anyone would spend money for it. The road will be rarely used and would lead nowhere.

In order to save time, Höller does not tell the man anything about the music experts and the heavy traffic that will soon appear among the vines. The renovation is an absolute necessity! he says, whereupon the foreman pulls a sheet from a pad and begins to calculate. He scratches figures on paper for a few minutes, then he names a price; the amount surprises Höller. If he tries to bargain, he could lose valuable time, thinks Höller and he accepts, whereupon the man takes a bottle of liquor from the first aid kit and presents two full glasses. He would talk to his supervisor; they could begin the work in a few days.

On the way back, partly because he barely has to pedal, Höller thinks about the *Fantasy*. Sentences from Schubert's book come to mind. His piano style is orchestral and vocal at the same time ... He had probably never had a grand piano, had his short life long struggled with inferior pianos and so he shaped his head into a piano according to his own terms ... If he stops pedalling in front of the town hall, he can certainly roll to the piazza ... In the Fantasy the piano would be so consistently transformed into an orchestra, as hitherto had been unprecedented ...

He leans the caretaker's wife's bicycle against the wall in front of the bar. I will guard your bike, Signor Brendel, says the boy. Höller slips him a bill and notes that the boy has a darker skin colour than the other children in Castelnuovo.

Still in the doorway, the old men from the farm notice him; the speaker calls out to him that there was no news about

Giuseppe. Giuseppe has returned to life. He no longer thinks about death and talks only about his masculinity. There is no prospect of his bed …

The owner appears from behind the coffee machine and barks at the old men not to bother the guests with their meaningless chatter. Whereupon the old man sits at Höller's table. Will you allow it? Without waiting for Höller's approval he continues to speak, whispering now quite close to Höller's ear, who breathes in the old man's odour, then feels for a few moments like a touch of nausea is rising in him; but it retreats when he backs away a little from the old man and smokes a cigarette.

One should not take everything that the owner is saying literally, he whispers to him with a conspiratorial look; the owner was a poor fool. For years his wife had cheated on him; the whole town knew it, but he did not want to see the truth. Like most *cornuti*, those horned jackasses, he trusted his wife and accepted the most stupid lies from her. Everyone had luck with Marietta, the old and the young. Even the one-legged Gianluca had landed in bed with her. With his wooden leg, he climbed up the stairs to the first floor while the innkeeper served Cappuccini and Chianti on the ground floor and the boy wrote his school essays and arithmetic in the bar. Recently she had left him and the boy, with one day's notice, because of a slick insurance agent from Siena …

Höller, who moved even further away from the old man, no longer listens to him, because he has been whispering since he began to talk about the owner's wife … Höller thinks about the word *cornuto*, and notes that he does not know how often Sophie cheated on him. Then he remembers a few of his own affairs, ridiculous escapades, of which he cannot say whether they were ever anything more than a helpless confirmation of his masculinity.

When Sophie established her office and received advice from a section chief of the ministry, he had assumed the lead lawyer was more than her mentor. He had he never discussed it with her, probably out of embarrassment about what to do if his suspicions were confirmed.

You must forget about Giuseppe's bed! he hears the old man beside him, who he has been ignoring for a few moments. He is not interested in that, Höller calms the man, who draws a deep breath of relief and wants to return to his friends' table. Höller holds him back by the upper arm, orders wine and talks about the emptiness, about the lack of responsibilities, and about the fact that it is wrong to rob people of his age of all their ambitions.

The old man nods uncertainly, drinks quickly, looks at his friends and has no idea what Höller is driving at.

He must not frighten the man, thinks Höller, and imagines him in the black usher's uniform. A new haircut, a careful shave, there is no doubt: with a few adjustments, he will make a perfect usher.

I will invite you and your friends to the barbershop! Höller says, and the old man looks at him with a stunned expression.

But for whatever reason would you want us …

A sudden idea, says Höller. Talk to your friends!

A little later they walk through the piazza. Höller in front, the old man and his friends close behind him. At the end of the line, the boy pushes the caretaker's wife's bicycle.

The barber stands in front of his shop, bored, but immediately grows busy and praises his own skills in lengthy baroque rhetoric, after Höller has paid for five haircuts and shaves. He has learned his trade, what is called a trade is his art, in Florence. And not in some suburban shop, but in the first salon on the Piazza Repubblica with Maestro Panucci. And, in regard to the art of hairstyling, one could compare it with Verdi or Montale; one thinks of music or poetry. And the art of hairstyling is absolutely comparable to music or the art of writers. Even with painting and sculpture, and with architecture; isn't the art of hairstyling architecture for the head? The poetry of music flowing through the hair?

The old men look at each other perplexed, from time to time a questioning look at Höller, who stares at his watch for several moments and hopes by doing so to remind the hairdresser of his work. The spokesman for the old men whispers in his ear, the hairdresser was a braggart; he would let himself be shot in the head if Francesco had ever worked in Florence. He had come from Buonconvento to Castelnuovo, alleging that his father had been an elementary school teacher there. But who cares about the father of a village barber? The old barber had recruited him many years ago, it was said, and not because he had mastered his craft so well, but because he had shortened the waiting period for the customers with Verdi arias. Years ago he was still endowed with a pleasant tenor voice, but he had drowned it in massive amounts of liquor, after the old barber had died and he had inherited the shop.

Five customers at the same time, says the hairdresser; that is a sensation in Castelnuovo. Naturally the customers in Florence would have to spend weeks trying to get an appointment, but one cannot compare the two places with each other.

And what is the reality today? he cries, and seizes Höller's forearm, holds it and waits for a response.

He was concerned with music, says Höller, and wrenches

himself from the hairdresser's grasp; he did not know anything about haircuts and fashion in general.

Look at the young men today, just once! the barber cries, and the old men wince. Some of them let their hair grow wild and fall to the shoulders, the others shave their empty heads bald; they don't use a barber but at best a pair of shears ... The boy rings the bicycle bell a few times and reminds the chatty barber that he must continue working.

The shop, Höller notices, is tiny and dark; inside it offers just enough space for one customer. The barber places his chairs outside and talks again about his *Florentine period*, and, in a tone that a singer would use, he speaks about his time at La Scala. Maestro Panucci had placed the greatest emphasis on comprehensive training for his apprentices, taught them not only the use of the comb and scissors, which most of his so-called peers were satisfied with. Therefore, his instruction took place not only in his salon, but also at the Uffizi, where Panucci went with his apprentices once a week, into the academy or into the picture gallery of the Palazzo Pitti, where they spent hours looking at the hairstyles in the paintings and made sketches. A barber who has not taken in Botticelli, Raphael and Michelangelo, was not a hairdresser, but an ordinary clipper ...

Finally, the chatty barber gets to work and calls the first customer inside. After a short time, that one returns and takes a vacant chair, while the next one disappears into the shop. Höller walks up and down in front of them and examines their heads closely. He imagines the entrance to the concert hall and the men with their new hair-styles beside these doors. When he also imagines the uniforms and caps, he is reassured. These men fit fine into the picture he has imagined. And Brendel will have no objection to them. Again and again, one of them takes his hat from his head and strokes the palm of his hand over the trimmed hair; they also feel their chin and cheeks.

Höller and the spokesman for the old men agree on a meeting halfway between the farm and the bar. They would come, he says, although he could not explain why they must meet outside …

Because of everyone's curiosity, Höller interrupts him. We will be discussing important things. Among the vines we will not be disturbed.

Höller sits in the tower listening to the *Fantasy* and thinks about the sensation in town, when the construction equipment comes rolling on chain wheels toward the community hall and begins tearing down the walls. An enormous dust cloud will pass over the houses. And the fields and vineyards.

He imagines how the people will gather together, because they cannot explain the noise and destruction. Some may fear that the machines will not only overturn the town hall, but once that is levelled, will continue to the centre of town and attack their homes. They call for the *carabinieri*, who drive up in their blue Alfa and calm the angry crowd: The demolition is approved by the Mayor and only affects the parish hall, where a concert hall will be erected in its place …

Why do we need a concert hall in Castelnuovo? a few of them ask. Until now the town hall has been good enough for all the evenings of folk music; none of the musicians and not one member of the audience have ever complained about the town hall.

The demolition is approved, say the *carabinieri*; there is no risk to the other houses!

Will people take sides against me, Höller deliberates, when, instead of their horrible town hall, they get a perfect concert hall?

Voices in the front garden. Höller looks out of the tower window. Two of the caretaker's children are standing in the yard with baskets. Our mother sent us with your lunch, they call up, and place the baskets by the front door. Later, when he warms the minestrone, Höller is confident. If the Mayor approves the construction, the people will agree.

Because the pressure in his head will not subside after the second tablet, Höller swallows a sleeping pill, even though the doctors have impressed upon him that he should not take this together with the analgesic drug. Höller closes the shutters in the bedroom and lies down on the bed. With closed eyes, he tries to eliminate the roar in his head and, since this does not succeed, he tries to find out what rhythm the rising and falling pain will obey. Later, after he has long since abandoned his futile attempts and knows that the tumour cannot be outwitted this afternoon, he sees Brendel and Schubert sitting at a piano. They play waltzes, to which Sophie is dancing in a deserted ballroom. Schubert's eyes circle behind thick glasses.

Continue! Brendel demands. The women will come. Listen to the waltz; they will come. They will run through the aisles, each one will try to pass the one in front of her. They will be standing in the hall in white dresses with colourful ribbons. A yearning waltz, which causes the fingers of all the Schubert enthusiasts who play along with the music to grow moist, and the excitement to drum against the skull in three-quarter time. With bass drums and trumpets. And a staccato bass from the grand piano, which flies in daring festoons through the ball room, the piano bench on which Höller now sees himself sitting, like a dragon's tail trailing behind him. All of the women disappear with Schubert and Brendel. The Waltzes have been played. Höller fumbles through the Fantasy. With numb fingers, at a snail's pace. He calls for Brendel's hands. Brendel must send him the hands. Airmail express. For without these marvellous hands the *Fantasy* will stumble back into the strings and hide itself in the grand piano …

Höller knows that while they are working on the road he will not be able to think clearly in La Torre. He believes that he is one step ahead and he wants to write down what he came up with after thinking for several minutes, but the hellish noise of the construction equipment is destroying his thoughts. Even with the windows closed, the steamroller rumbles through his head, where there is now a terrible chaos because of the excavation. So close to the goal he cannot be tempted to any inattention, Höller resolves.

First, he needs to find safety from the chain links of the steamroller for every single thought. It is all merely a question of organisation. Höller looks into his head and reorganises his thoughts. He combines the ones that have to do with the *Fantasy* into groups and deposits them in a protected place at the edge of his mind. There, they cannot be rolled over by the construction equipment.

He is progressing slowly because of the noise and vibrations, but after several hours he can sit back and relax. All the important thoughts are ordered and brought to safety.

After he recovers from the effort and swallows another painkiller, Höller goes down the hill to the caretaker's house and halfway down he meets the construction crew. The foreman greets him and explains the procedures. There have been no unforeseeable difficulties, the man says, and that the work could proceed quickly. If Höller is prepared to pay a bonus for overtime, the paving could be completed the next day.

Höller agrees without hesitation, and the foreman warns him away from the scalding steam rising from the cauldron of asphalt. If he gets too close, it could burn his eyes.

In the courtyard of the caretaker's house is the *carabinieri's* blue Alfa. A young officer sits behind the wheel smoking. Outside the entrance to the wine cellar, the Inspector talks with the caretaker. When he notices Höller, he runs after him and asks to speak. An official discussion, he adds, and puts on his cap.

He is in a hurry, says Höller, and tries to shake off the policeman, who, however, keeps up with him; and it is completely obvious that he does not know how to begin the *official discussion*. He talks about the road work and the special location of La Torre on the hill. And in front of the entrance to the caretaker's house: How long will you stay in Castelnuovo? When Höller remains silent, he changes his tone of voice, asks about Höller's intentions and whether they are of a business nature or private.

The police language makes Höller listen attentively. He knows that he should not mention the *Fantasy*, not before the last ambiguities have been addressed and the crucial discussion with the Mayor has taken place. He was here, Höller says, to have a rest from his business. Then he describes his factory to the Inspector, adding a few technical details about the production of air conditioner systems and those car brands that have parts from his factory, because he hoped the man would then lose any interest in him.

He will not be taken for a fool! the Inspector roars at him, and Höller winces; he cannot explain what in his statement has aroused the wrath of the police officer. He has only talked about his factory and the circuits for air conditioning in German cars.

This is no longer a private conversation, the official interrupts Höller's deliberations, but an interrogation in a police investigation. The young *carabiniere* is suddenly standing beside him, seizes his forearm and requests that he follow him into the caretaker's house.

The caretaker's wife is standing in the vestibule with the two youngest children, who do not attend school yet. The boy aims at Höller with a plastic gun from behind his mother's back; the girl hides her face in her mother's skirt. They've cleaned up the dining room, whispers the woman; the interrogation could take place in the dining room.

The policemen demand that Höller take a seat at the table and go to the window, where they talk something over together briefly, and soon after take a seat across from him. The young *carabiniere* places a notepad on the table; both take off their caps; then the Inspector asks Höller detailed questions. The younger man has trouble taking notes; Höller must spell names again and again, and he sees how impatient the Inspector is growing.

Do you know Florentin Raddu? he asks, barely audible.

When Höller says that he has never heard the name in his life, the Inspector jumps up and shouts that he would arrest Höller immediately if he has already answered the first question with a lie.

Again this pressure in his head, the slight dizziness that makes the images quiver. Höller reaches in his jacket pocket and holds the bag containing the painkillers; he knows he must not yield to the pain now or the *carabinieri* will think he is trying to evade their questions.

You have been seen with the boy again and again! On the piazza in front of the lawyer's office; and in front of the post office. Yesterday he pushed your bike across the piazza. There are witnesses! the Maresciallo says. Think carefully about your next answers!

Of course he knew the boy, Höller says, but that is already saying too much; he did not really know the boy, did not know his name, which he had just heard for the first time. The boy had been following him since the day he came to Castelnuovo. He was constantly popping up out of nowhere and offering his services. From the very beginning, it had been clear to him that he could not shake off the boy, so he had accepted his small services and paid him for them.

The *carabiniere* throws his superior a questioning look, asking if he should continue to take notes, and requests that Höller go on.

The boy was probably caught stealing, Höller thinks, and now the *carabinieri* want to use his statement to complete their picture of the little thief because they hope he can help them with details.

Whatever crime the boy has committed, Höller says, he knew nothing about it, for he had remained a stranger to him like the other children. All that was noticeable to him was the insolence and the obstinacy with which he had thrust upon him his services.

Florentin Raddu has not committed a crime, the Inspector says after a long pause. The boy is dead. Someone found him in the early morning hours, struck dead in a ditch a few hundred yards from here. With a gaping wound to his head. We also know that he was not killed where we found him. The boy's parents live in a camp for Roma people on the outskirts of Siena and have brought their son to Castelnuovo every morning to beg and picked him up again in the evening. But yesterday, he did not appear at the agreed meeting point.

Höller is silent. The Inspector calls for the caretaker's wife and asks her for three cups of coffee. Höller think of the time he will lose if he gets involved in a murder investigation; knows also that his time belongs exclusively to the *Fantasy*; any distraction can mean failure.

Could it not also have been, the Inpsector asks over coffee in such a friendly tone that it alarmed Höller immediately, that you could no longer endure being constantly harassed by the boy?

He resigned himself to the presence of the boy long ago, says Höller. Besides, it would have been easy to get rid of him. And it had not amounted to anything for him to slip the boy a few Euros.

Nevertheless we all know these days, the Maresciallo insists, that one cannot even bear the familiar stuff. A sudden rage, perhaps, far removed from any intention, you create space for your anger by striking out. Then, without ever having even thought it was possible, you are holding a stone in your hand, strike before you've even noticed that a deadly weapon … You strike and only now discover what you have done, without …

Or the irritations that, from one moment to the next, are no longer irritations, but grow quite suddenly into a threat. You push back against a dangerous assailant, because you may really for a moment fear for your life; you push with all your might and the attacker stumbles backwards, surprised that he cannot catch his fall with his arms, hitting his head exactly where there is by chance the edge of a wall, a stairway landing, or merely a sharp stone ...

Whatever has happened to the boy, he had seen the boy for the last time in front of the barbershop, where he had looked after the caretaker's wife's bicycle, Höller says with a certainty that silences the Inspector, and feels safe for a time because he knows that the *carabinieri* have nothing that connects him to the crime. The boy had vanished long before he left the piazza with the men from the farm. There were witnesses.

The young officer closes his notebook and goes outside. In the yard, the Inspector asks why Höller is paving a road that does not belong to him. And when Höller remains silent: if you constantly do things that are not understood by the people here, you will really provoke the curiosity of the villagers. Who can understand the fact that you spend an enormous sum to pave a road that is rarely used by the farm workers? What are your intentions? people naturally ask themselves in this case, and watch your every move. Which they would have done already, after you started meeting regularly at the bar with residents of the nursing home. What secrets are discussed at these meetings? Where does this strange man go again and again, without leaving information, and appearing a few days later without saying a word about his absence? Why is it that every time he appears on the piazza, he is accompanied by a Roma boy?

How long will Höller remain in Castelnuovo? the Inspector wants to know, and, before he gets into the car, he says that the next day Höller must come to the prefecture to sign minutes of the hearing.

Before he makes his way back, Höller asks the caretaker's wife for a glass of water. He knows that without another pain-killer, he cannot manage the trip. Not today, and after this excitement. With his clumsy attempt to quickly find a culprit, in order to return to his usual idleness, the Inspector has marginalised the *Fantasy*. He will not make a single step forward with his plans today. And the pain reminds him that time is working against him.

When Höller notices the woman's questioning gaze, he assures her that everything has been cleared up, and the Inspector has withdrawn his accusations. It is probably the same everywhere when something terrible happens: strangers are the first to be suspected. In any case, after the trial he was safe from further accusations and please also let the caretaker know. The arrival of the *carabinieri* had changed nothing, all the agreements they had made remained in effect. It would be best if they would forget the bad comedy that had played out in the caretaker's house that afternoon, and not say another word about it.

The way back is actually torture, again and again, Höller must lean against a cypress trunk, relax and wait with his eyes closed until a sudden attack of vertigo has subsided. When he comes up to La Torre, the tri-color cat comes running towards him and rubs purring against the leg of his trousers. He puts slices of Mortadella on a plate for her in front of the stairway landing and sits down beside the cat, who continues to purr while she eats. After she has cleaned herself, she rubs up against Höller's legs again and lets him stroke her back. For more than half an hour he fondles the cat, who has fallen with pleasure into a trance-like state and turns her body towards him where she wants to be petted. When the cat walks slowly across the yard, Höller feels his breathing grow more regular and he is ready again to think about the music. And if he can no longer work on the *Fantasy* this evening, he will listen to music. He will put on Schubert; certainly not the *Fantasy*, but the *Impromptus, Opus 90 and 142*, played by Brendel. He will listen to them in the tower and regain his confidence.

AGAINST THE ADVICE of his doctor, Höller has taken a sleeping pill with the painkillers and has slept until morning. No panic attack, no palpitations, no nausea, no circulatory collapse followed; on the contrary, Höller cannot remember the last time he woke up so relaxed. After he has fed the cat in the yard, he is on his way to Castelnuovo. He wants to sign the minutes of the absurd hearing as quickly as possible in order to absorb himself exclusively in the *Fantasy*.

Again, he borrows the bike from the caretaker's wife. The slight slope of the road is not difficult; Höller has not felt so strong in weeks. Healthy, he thinks, and strikes the word immediately, because the deadly enemy is in his head, even if he has outwitted it this morning.

From the young *carabiniere*, who is standing guard in front of the prefecture, he learns that the minutes cannot be signed until ten o'clock. A slight delay, he assures himself, and goes to the bar in the piazza, where the artisans and employees crowd in to have a morning coffee before they start their work. The guests especially crowd around the counter, because they pay less for the coffee if they stand than they would if they drink it at the tables.

As the guests notice Höller, they begin to talk quietly. A couple of them put their heads together, and Höller suspects that they are now talking about him. Probably adventurous speculation about the murder of the Roma boy and his involvement in the crime. Some of them will probably see him as the culprit and will be surprised that he has not been arrested immediately following the interrogation; undoubtedly everyone present knows all about that.

When the owner comes to his table with the caffè doppio and Höller remains silent, he apologises for the harassment and asks what had resulted from the interrogation on the day before; he did not wish to impose, but it was better for everyone present if everything was clarified before people caused damage with their talk that was impossible to repair.

You have not served coffee to a murderer, says Höller, and orders a grappa. And in an hour he would sign the minutes that note his innocence, he says, and sees that the owner immediately reports the news at the counter, where he hopes to see the disappointment in some faces when they learn that they have not had their morning coffee with a killer.

Along with the schnapps, the owner brings the local newspaper to the table and says that an article about the murder has already appeared and it also mentions Höller. While he reads, he can see from the corner of his eye that most of the guests are watching him. Of course they want to assess his response to the article in order to make new speculations about him: a twitching around the mouth, perhaps an indignant hand gesture.

After only a few sentences, Höller knows that the journalist has few facts to report, and takes refuge using lurid phrases to describe general terms and assumptions. He writes about the problem of nomadic camps on the edge of the large cities, about children who are forced to beg and steal by their unscrupulous parents. And the fact that the prefectures of some major cities are planning to create a registry with fingerprints of the Roma children who are apprehended while begging or stealing, and that the Leftist parties and the European Union speak against it, he notes; that in order to solve the problem of the *clandestini* with a few sentences, they end in a conviction that all illegal immigrants should be expelled immediately. Höller reads little about the dead boy, Florentin Raddu, and about himself there is only the sentence that in connection with the brutal murder a foreign businessman who was staying for several weeks in Castelnuovo had been questioned. The journalist had not even researched his name, Höller notes, and continues to browse. He scans the headlines and finally comes across an article that helps him forget his anger.

Because the tenor of a provincial opera house sang the wrong notes again and again, which the audience did not forgive, although it was known to be particularly uncritical – was even considered the most uncritical in the entire country – he thought of suicide. Most of all because he had learned nothing of value during his insufficient voice training at a conservatory of dubious reputation. He lacked any perspective for a successful life after the opera. And he was not attractive, so he could not hope to be supported by a rich widow.

He was once again in "Rigoletto", merciless as usual, but on this evening, having got lost in the notes, it was clear to him that suicide was the only way out of his artistic and human dilemma. He adroitly loaded a prop revolver, which he had wrangled from the weak-minded property caretaker of the provincial opera house under false pretences.

Even before he put on his make-up, he put the barrel to his head, but then sneezed just at the moment he pulled the trigger. So the bullet missed its target and struck the dressing room door.

Because he believed himself to be dead, or merely out of fear from the blast, the tenor fainted. He tumbled off the chair and took such a terrible fall that he died with a broken neck before the first curious onlookers stormed his dressing room.

Then, the author makes assumptions about what he calls the particular danger to tenors. They were the celebrated heroes of the opera houses, but would also be mercilessly destroyed by an audience lusting after high notes, who, even in the smallest theatres, will only accept a top level performance from the singer. And then he reports another act of desperation by a tenor, which occurred some years earlier:

A young tenor in Pisa, who sang not one single false note during the rehearsal, was overcome with nervousness from one day to the next before every performance. He stumbled through the notes, forgetting all the parts of his text; he could not even remember his position on the stage, and was booed mercilessly. Sometimes the role was passed on to the understudy, and the theatre management published medical reports, which attempted to explain the tenor's indisposition. With a mysterious throat disease or the death of his beloved mother. Even so, the singer's only true friend, a parakeet, had been lost to cardiac arrest. To cure him, the management sent the singer to Sardinia, from where he confirmed in regular phone calls that he felt free of all stress. His return to the stage was planned; the first performance after his month-long absence was announced; the ticket sales were very satisfactory. On the evening before his return flight the singer, without leaving a farewell letter, which would have provided a plausible explanation for his behaviour, fell from his hotel room on the seventh floor. A romantic, unrequited love, the press speculated; no one spoke of the false notes with which he ruined each aria ...

THE SIGNATURE at the Prefecture is merely a formality, quickly dealt with. A young officer offers to arrange a translator for him if Höller does not understand everything that was recorded in the minutes. Once Höller has signed, the officer says that with this signature the matter was settled and he can expect no further inquiry.

HE HAS BEEN free from pain for more than a day, Höller determines reassuredly as he makes his way to the meeting with the old men from the farm. Of course he knows that this does not mean improvement. But the fact that he did not have to increase the painkillers again after the excitement he has endured helps him to forget the inevitable.

To make sure he does not run into the arms of the rowdy caretaker again, Höller walks between the pines along the side of the road. A quick glance at his watch shows him that he will reach the agreed meeting place before the old men. A little later he has found the ideal place in a clearing for the meeting with his future ushers, who, with their new haircuts, must certainly already be on their way. They probably cannot imagine the reason for the meeting, and are making the wildest speculations. Realising that he paid for the haircuts will calm them down and prove that he is their friend.

And then there are six of them standing in the clearing. Giuseppe came along, says their spokesman; he also wants a new haircut and would like to pay attention to his looks again, because he hopes to regain his manhood soon.

Look! Giuseppe shouts and extends the crumpled page from a magazine towards Höller. Read! We are saved!

Höller observes Giuseppe, his looks, his way of standing and walking. A few minor corrections, a neat hair cut, and then he can be accepted as an usher.

The newspaper! Giuseppe shouts.

We must not lose any time, Höller says. It will take several minutes for me to read the article.

First the newspaper! the spokesman for the old men demands.

So Höller begins to read, to avoid even the slightest discord: *Il primo Esperimento Risale oltre a cent ' anni fa: il 1 ° giugno 1889 il grande fisiologo settantaduenne Brown Sequard communicò a Parigi, durante una seduta della società di biologia, di aver riacquistato in pochi giorni forza, un estratto iniettato acquoso di testicolo di cane. E anche se, ancora oggi, nessuno è riuscito a capire come quella iniezione abbia potuto produrre gli effetti descritti, le ricerche non si sono mai interrotte ...*

After a few sentences he knows that it is the article about absurd rejuvenation cures, the one the old man talked about in the bar a few weeks ago, which culminates in the description of an allegedly successful experiment. A scientist from the 19th century explains the remarkable rejuvenation of subjects with a treatment in which the old men were injected with the testicular fluid of dogs.

And do you believe this story? Höller asks.

Unconditionally! the old men shout in unison.

And why are you showing me this report?

The old men put their heads together and whisper. Because, their spokesman says after a short time, you have to get the injections! You are powerful. You can run after a dog and anaesthetise him. Because no dog is going to let anybody near his balls while he is conscious.

Impossible! Höller shouts, louder than intended, and the old men wince. We must not waste time with obscure experiments.

Then, says Giuseppe, there will be no meeting!

Remember what is at stake! Höller cries. But the old men know nothing about his plans, so his admonishment does not impress them. In their faces he sees that they have committed themselves.

Think of the haircuts. The shaves! He makes a last attempt.

They are worthless without the injections! Giuseppe says. First the assurance, then the discussion!

Höller knows that he must not put the *Fantasy* at risk because of the preposterous mood of his ushers. And certainly the men would react differently if they already knew that he will appoint them as ushers. So he relents; he would grant their wish, but it could take weeks before the funds are available.

That did not matter, says Giuseppe, and the men sit down on a pile of lumber.

While Höller talks about the *Fantasy*, they stare with boredom into the emptiness. He speaks of the ultimate music, and they are probably thinking of their masculinity and the fact that they will once again succeed in penetrating a woman. See themselves running after young girls with strong legs and tight skin.

They anticipate the arousal and begin to move back and forth on the woodpile. They become attentive only when Höller describes their uniforms and the brightly lit lobby they will be able to go through in them.

And now I need to see how you move! Höller says.

Perplexed glances from the old men.

After some hesitation, his ushers walk across the clearing. Giuseppe stays back, because he limps.

Stop! Höller shouts, and his ushers pause. What happened to your leg? he asks the one who is limping.

His Libyan leg is predicting a bad weather front, the man says. And before Höller can prevent it, the old man starts to talk about his Libyan leg, probably mentally shipping himself off for the thousandth time as a young recruit to the African campaign; he talks about the heat and the thirst that robbed most of the soldiers of their sanity. He talks about the endless expanse of the desert, about the night and the terrible cold which can freeze the mind. He talks about the tanks and trucks stuck in the desert sand, and of the fact that in the desert any notion of distance is lost; after days in the desert a metre was no longer distinguishable from a kilometre. Finally his battalion got into an ambush; they were fired upon by an invisible enemy, everyone running in order to find a safe cover from which they fired back, in the direction of the machine gun fire. And suddenly he sees a lower leg lying next to him while he reloads; he thinks the grenade has hit his neighbour until he sees, (without which he would have felt only a slight pain), that it was indeed his own leg, next to him in the desert sand … But his Libyan leg probably saved his life, because they sent him home by sea in a hospital ship, while hardly any of his friends ever saw their homeland again. Still in the hospital in Sicily, they had customised a wooden leg for him, with which he now stalks through his life, but he has never forgotten his Libyan leg. And his Libyan leg still thinks of him, informs him when the weather changes, and is more reliable than the weather report on the television …

With a walk like that you cannot be an usher …

We will only wear your uniforms as a team! the spokesman for the old men interrupts Höller, who wants to avoid any confrontation.

We will work on your leg, he reassures the man. On the important evening, your Libyan leg will not be noticed!

THE FURTHER ALONG HE gets in his preparations, the more details whir through Höller's mind, where the traffic of his thoughts prevails like rush hour on the ring roads of major cities. Observations follow other observations; new ideas suddenly take the lead and push others ruthlessly aside, and it is inevitable with this density of thought traffic that shunts occur again and again at critical points when a new idea, disregarding the rules of the right of way, swerves and touches the thought in front of it, both of which cause extensive damage to the remaining traffic for a considerable time.

Höller knows that countless details of the work must be dealt with; the planned sequence of events must not be jeopardised. A careless detail can thwart the *Fantasy*. And Höller also knows that he cannot do all the work himself. He is performing the preliminary work for the music; he will lead the negotiations with the Mayor. But who is supervising the work on the concert hall? Who is training the ushers? Who is taking care of the travelling music experts? And finally, the most delicate task: Who is organising the transportation for the grand piano from the Bösendorfer concert hall to Castelnuovo? The arrogant board of directors of the Viennese music association has not even answered the first inquiry or the second, and will perhaps even reject the third without reason as inconceivable. Finally, a typical Viennese characteristic will prevail: Greed! In combination with a second characteristic: Vienna's addiction to meaning. After the fourth letter, it will be suggested that under certain conditions it will be possible to transport the grand piano in the Bösendorfer concert hall from Vienna to Italy for a single concert, an international musical sensation. If this point is reached, it's just a question of giving the music association's executive board the feeling that they have extorted an inflated price during their negotiations. Höller knows that the Viennese don't care about the grand piano from the Bösendorfer concert hall; it has become unplayable because of an unfortunate accident during transportation. They immediately ran to the Ministry of Art and received the promise from an unsuspecting politician: in order not to jeopardise Vienna's status as the capital of music, he would provide a comparable grand piano for the Bösendorfer concert hall. But Höller cannot deal with these practical things. For this, he must hire a secretary.

LATER, WHEN HE crosses the piazza, perplexed because he knows no one in this country who would be suitable for this task, he remembers the professor, who knows nothing about music, but wants to leave the *pension*, and is the only man in the place who has the self-assurance and the knowledge that is required of a music secretary.

In order to speak to the professor he must go to the *pension*, where there is a risk that he will run into Signora Carmela, and she will press him with questions and allegations concerning his hasty exodus. He does not want to indulge the woman in this scene; he will wait at the side entrance of the church until she goes to the market, where she completes the purchases for lunch each day. When she leaves the *pension*, he will have scarcely an hour to convince the professor.

Höller finds the professor later, in the breakfast room, over the *Corriere*. The state is falling apart, he says, and shows Höller a picture of the ever-grinning Prime Minister. Insane people had elected these criminals for the third time, and that probably says everything about the state of mind of the voters, who have to be either completely stupid or criminal like their Prime Minister.

He does not want to talk about politics this morning. Höller tries to calm the man, who immediately interrupts him and asks what he wants to talk about. But Höller must not answer, because the professor could very well imagine what preoccupied him. Of course he would like to talk about some *andante* in some sonata; the state is falling apart, but the Lord is not interested in music experts; it was only important whether or not any pianist played a damned *andante* too quickly and completely disfigured a sonata ...

Pardon my agitation, the professor says after a short time, but I find it harder every day to watch how this government degenerates more and more and is now compared in some foreign newspapers to South American banana republics. Höller waves it off, which reassures the professor, who inquires about Sophie. Do you know how much your wife has always excited me?

Then he talks about the country's leading politician, who has sold all the assets, and concludes by asking whether or not Höller knows of a civilised country whose Prime Minister was accused in numerous proceedings and the only reason he could not be convicted was because he has been assured complete immunity by his delegate majority through a disgraceful law.

You can participate, Höller says, in the fight against the loss of values, and establish a connection between threatened values and music, which is also threatened by thoughtless interpretations. When he sees the professor's interest, he asks about the lady from Milan who had recently had surgery, and paints a bleak picture of the stupid conversations that awaited him, if he did not leave the *pension* and move to La Torre. And when can he begin the job as music secretary?

I will have my bags packed in fifteen minutes, says the professor, and folds up the pages of the *Corriere*.

On the caretaker's bicycle, Höller returns to the *pension*, where the professor is already waiting with two shabby suitcases. Has he changed his mind, Höller asks, when he notices the tired look of the man, who only shakes his head and later says that while packing, he had been surprised that so little was left of his life that he could put it into two suitcases. Of course his wife and her lawyer had cheated him in the divorce, but he had not expected that his whole life would fit into two bags.

Höller wants to avoid being discovered by Signora Carmela, fears her reproaches, when within a few days the second permanent lodger leaves her *pension*, and suggested that they leave. But the professor will not let himself be distracted from his memories and talks of the messy divorce battle that his wife had dragged him into. While his wife (his junior by many years), was taking advice from a cunning lawyer in this fight, he could only hope from the start that as a lone soldier in an unequal confrontation, his defeat would be as lenient as possible. But even this hope was destroyed after a few minutes in the courtroom, when he realised that the judge was on the side of his wife and did not even try to hide the illegality. The law is the same for everyone: you read that in all the courtrooms in the country; and this sentence was not meant under any circumstances to be ironic. But sitting in front of this sentence the libidinous caricature of a divorce court judge had made a judgment that agreed on all points with his wife and even brought him almost to literally begging. To this very day, he can still see the man's hungry eyes gazing at his wife's cleavage or under the table at her crossed legs, while he tried desperately to explain his role in this sexual comedy. He described for the court scenes of infidelity in detail and at the time had the impression that the judge was listening to him attentively. But now he knows that he was only interested in the erotic excesses of his wife and probably imagined himself as one of his wife's lovers.

A withered up secretary noted his arguments, but after the meeting probably stuffed them into file folders unread.

Höller and the professor mount the two small suitcases onto the caretaker's wife's bicycle with straps and push it across the piazza by walking on either side, one hand on the handlebars, the second one on the suitcases. Children follow them until they reach the city limits, taunting them from a safe distance, shouting insults at them and mocking their movements.

Giovinezza, giovinezza, primavera di Bellezza, the professor reads on the wall of a house, and asks Höller whether or not he knows what the words mean. He can translate it into his own language, Höller answers, whereupon the professor interrupts him and roars that a simple translation will probably make him think of a folk song or an adolescent love letter. But the words on the wall came from a song by the fascists, probably sprayed there a few weeks ago by one of those skinheads, who bullied the neighbourhood on their motorcycles. No one can be found to paint over this mess, and that is the real scandal. But what could you expect from a country that sold wine bottles with a picture of Mussolini on the label? And not surreptitiously under the table, but legally, and in public.

They continue in silence, and have to stop again and again to take a deep breath and gather strength. Fortunately, the work of the road is completed, thinks Höller, and cannot imagine that they would have managed to push the bicycle with the suitcases up the hill of the cart path. Bathed in sweat, they come to La Torre, where the professor takes a room on the ground floor, while Höller wants to live in the tower. There he is near the *Fantasy*.

IN THE EVENING HÖLLER SITS in the tower with the professor and familiarises him with his duties as a music secretary, while the *Fantasy* plays from the speakers. When Höller presses the replay button, it starts again with the beginning chords, just a few seconds after the last note has died away.

Höller describes the ushers and their idiosyncrasies to his secretary; he also acts them out for him to the sounds of the *Fantasy*, going into details about each one, even imitating Giuseppe's Libyan leg. The professor agrees with him immediately when he says that no one should be able to notice on the important evening that one of the ushers is lame.

I have tamed hordes of unruly students, the professor reassures him; so I will deal with your ushers, too!

It is more difficult to familiarise the man with the language of music experts. Therefore Höller resolves, in what his father would have called a *drastic measure*, to read musical reviews and excerpts from musician's biographies to the professor into the morning hours. When, with the first light, he leaves the tower, Höller is certain that he will be able to handle his duties as his music secretary.

RAIN AND FOG in the morning. His usher's Libyan leg was right. Höller looks out from the tower and encounters an impenetrable wall. Nothing of the place can be recognised. The meeting with the Mayor is imminent; he is sitting at his desk behind this smoke screen somewhere and does not realise that he will tear down the community hall.

When he reaches the ground floor, the professor has already

brewed coffee and has set the breakfast table. He sits across from Höller with bloodshot eyes, pouring coffee into the cups and he says, after he had returned to his room he had not gone to bed, but sat at the table and read musical texts.

For Schubert's piano music, as is only otherwise true for that of Liszt, Anton Rubinstein's words apply: the pedal is the soul of the piano. Without bountiful, controlled and highly imaginative use of the pedal, this music is reduced to the self-sufficiency of the far-too-piano-like, Höller's musical secretary cites while he smears white bread with butter.

Does Höller know that Arturo Benedetti Michelangeli had been a ski racer and a combat pilot? the professor asks as he washes the dishes and cups. When he sees Höller's surprised look he says, he had that night for the first time in his life delved into the personal history of pianists, and had learned amazing things during his reading. In their autobiographies, most of them wrote very little about music; they wrote about women and their relationships, about hotels, travel, and extravagant restaurants. Naturally in that short time, he was only able to read a few pages, but this reading had completely unsettled him. He associated an artist with men for whom nothing but their art existed, and now he had to repaint this picture, since one of them fires salvos from his machine-gun and the next racks his brains over the quality of the oysters in the haute cuisine restaurants of New York. While Höller remains silent, because he is thinking of Brendel and the *Fantasy*, and he knows that it would take hours to rebut the professor's prejudice, he asks: Did you know that the Prime Minister, who is one of the richest men in the world today and controls a media empire, was also a so-called artist? At the beginning of his distinguished career, this Pied Piper worked as a cocktail pianist on cruise ships ...

Maybe it was not a good idea, Höller interrupts his music secretary, to rush through books about music at such a frantic pace. He must only know the most important terms, in order to take care of the visiting music experts; his real tasks, however, are to provide the ushers with introductory training and to support him when it comes to negotiating with the authorities.

On the way to the tower, Höller thinks about his music secretary's perplexing sentences, and recognizes that it was unreasonable to subject the professor to the *drastic measure of music theory*. He had hopelessly overwhelmed him with his requirements, but the professor would have done anything to keep from having to return to the *pension*. He plays the *Fantasy* and, after the opening chords, he has demoted his music secretary to a simple secretary. Now he will no longer have to struggle with pianist combat pilots and Chinese prodigies who play every piece a shade faster, and without a single false note.

When he listens to the *Fantasy* for a second time, he remembers Sophie's surprise gift on his fiftieth birthday. After they had barely spoken to each other for weeks, because Sophie had once again concentrated exclusively on the crucial phase of an important trial, she announced to him one morning that she would not work the next two days. And the children would arrive; at last his *special day*, (she actually used this absurd formulation), must be celebrated properly. No sooner had she expressed this absurd sentence than Höller thought of a funeral, in which the role of the corpse was allotted to him.

He turns fifty and, as she must know after all the years they have spent together, he does not care about numbers; a *milestone* birthday meant just as little to him as any other. Höller tried to avert the inevitable. But even as he spoke, he realised that Sophie had planned everything down to the smallest detail, like the closing remarks during her trials.

Brendel has completed the *Fantasy* and Höller thinks that Sophie will no longer have the chance to think up awful things for his next *milestone* birthday.

On the evening before, Nathalie arrived at the villa and started, even before she had showered and rested after the flight, talking about her new project. She had turned to art, visual art. America was light years ahead of Europe. Europe is a faded memory; America is leading the direction. The art market looks only to America; you could forget Europe, excluding some auctions for nouveau riche Russian social climbers.

Höller's attempt to interrupt Nathalie by reminding her of the exertion of her journey, even of his *milestone* birthday, he recalled, failed miserably. He had been the one who had always insisted that she look for a serious pursuit, and now that she had found it, he showed no interest.

Tears flowed; she would take the next plane back to the States if she was only going to face this narrow-minded lack of understanding … Finally resigned, Höller apologised for his insensitivity and asked his daughter to continue her report.

She had, Nathalie explained, turned to the art of photography, because after a long search and countless attempts, she had found that this form was most consistent with her innermost being. A prestigious gallery in Los Angeles is already interested in her project, but this requires a deposit, which is due before the exhibition, and she anticipates that this will be paid by him. Then she named a horrendous sum that reduced Höller to silence.

After looking in Sophie's direction for help, it was clear that she would not support him against Nathalie's outrageous demand. It was not clear to him whether she took this attitude because she wanted to hurt him, or only because she wanted to forget her guilty conscience over the fact that she had never sacrificed her time for the children.

Where did the greatness of her photographic work lie, he asked without interest, thinking that the common denominator among his children was their love of money. The difference was that Clemens needed money to increase it, while Nathalie always found new ways to waste vast sums of money on absurd projects.

Los Angeles is an island of the famous, Nathalie began, and it is time to fuse art and everyday life into an inseparable whole!

Höller feared the worst, because anyone who is able to introduce their *life's work* with two platitudes of this kind, does not shy away from anything.

This *prestigious* California gallery owner was enthusiastic about her idea to photograph the contents of celebrities' rubbish bins and thereby elevate them to art. She does not doubt that the project would be implemented as soon as the money was deposited into the gallery's account, Nathalie said with a glance at Höller. Her only uncertainty concerned the point of view that she must choose for her pictures, for, as in all great art, her point of view must be correct. She vacillates between two possibilities: the first one was to lift the lids of the bins and photograph this view. But this decision would not work for her, because in this case only the uppermost layer of rubbish is visible to represent their characteristic personalities in their entirety. After she had brooded for several weeks, she was now leaning toward the second possibility. Before shooting, she would pour the contents of the bins into the street, and could get closer to the celebrities this way. But this method is not safe and raises a few questions. Who would pick up the rubbish from the street and put it back into the bin? She could find a student or an unemployed rock musician for that. But what to do if there was active resistance against her photographic forays? Or if some service personnel try to prevent her from emptying the bins, and the police threatened to ...

Höller had heard enough and left the room, accompanied by a withering look from Sophie and Nathalie's threat that she would explain her concept to him in greater detail in the morning. Which, fortunately, did not happen, because Clemens, who had arrived on the first flight from London, was sitting at breakfast when Höller entered the room, approached him with his inevitable *Dear Father*, embraced him, (which immediately made Höller suspicious), and said, *May I invite you*; inviting him to begin this holiday with him in a traditional café in the city centre.

During the taxi ride from the edge of town to the center, Höller wondered what it was about his son that disturbed him so much he would have liked to order the driver to turn around. In front of the Central Café he knew the reason when Clemens, who got out before him, waited for him beside the car. It was not the formal English that he spoke, but the black business suit, which should probably make him look like a successful businessman in Höller's eyes, but only lent him the charm of a Russian secret agent. Höller also found no plausible reason for the trip into town; he learned what it was when the waiter had taken their order. Sophie was preparing a surprise. Höller, then, like children on Christmas Eve, when the Christmas trees were decorated, must stay away from the villa so he did not discover the *big surprise* before it was time. And he had decided on the Central because the State Department officials drank their tea or coffee here.

While Höller thought about what Sophie might have concocted, Clemens seemed to have forgotten him. He constantly watched the entrance and could not hide his disappointment when there were only more Japanese or Italian tourists who entered the café. In between, he spoke of receiving British citizenship, which would make it easier for him to work as a lawyer on the island. Wouldn't that be difficult at his age? Höller asked. By no means, said Clemens; he must simply marry an English woman, best a young woman from a family steeped in tradition, which, in addition to a wife, would also provide the advantages of their connections. These old English families were constantly involved in litigation; he could earn enormous amounts in the shortest time which, if profitably invested, would guarantee complete independence after a few years.

Clemens suddenly jumped up and ran across the room to a table near the entrance, where a man whose most striking feature was his unmanageable, curly hair, had taken a seat. His son stood next to the table for a short time, then he sat down with the man and talked to him like an insurance agent that does not want to let a potential client slip through his claws.

He later said that the man was Dr. Bayerl, the deputy ambassador to Ukraine. To know such a man is *very important* these days; the east was an economic region for hope on an unprecedented scale. When they left the Café, Höller asked whether or not Clemens, in addition to British citizenship, would also like to receive it from the Ukraine; at this offence, he remained silent and did not speak again until they reached the moat around the city, when he suggested that they drink a glass of champagne at Meinl's before the return trip.

In front of the villa there was a delivery van for some catering company that also did work for the government, and Höller fled immediately to the library, where he read Brendel's *Reflections on Music*, until Sophie was standing in the door in an evening dress and asked him to change his clothes for the reception. So that was what Sophie had come up with for him on his *milestone* birthday: to supply a horde of more or less good acquaintances, who he went out of his way to avoid whenever he could.

Sophie supervised his preparations and forced him to wear the dinner jacket, when he had reached for a dark gray suit. It was an *official* reception and not a casual invitation to afternoon coffee; if he wanted to make her look bad, he ought to wear the traditional costume of his farmer director, then his old-fashioned appearance would be just perfect.

While he had been reading Brendel's book and had been thinking only about music, countless assistants had transformed the small park in front of the villa into a meadow with a party atmosphere of the worst kind. White tents stood on the edge of the lawn, where liveried servants stood behind enormous quantities of delicacies and exquisite beverages, prepared to satisfy the needs of the pampered guests. The climax of bad taste, however, was a plastic pavilion in the center; Höller had no idea what its function was, as he stood by Sophie at the top of the stairs and thought only of how he could escape this grotesque production. The guests were crowded together; the deep setting sun blinded Höller so he could not recognise any faces, and, only a few feet away from the others, he could just make out, as a last ally in the middle of countless enemies, his manager's traditional costume.

After he had been standing beside Sophie on the top of the

stairs for a few moments, the faceless crowd applauded, and Höller saw a figure in the bright backlight peel away from the mass and approach them. Only when the figure was standing directly in front of him, did he recognise the Minister of the Economy, with whom he had spoken briefly two or three times in the Ministry and who now greeted him like an old friend. After a tender handshake, which Höller thought would last forever, the politician turned to the faceless crowd, fished a sheet of paper from the inside pocket of his jacket and pulled out a speech, written of course by a junior secretary, and which the Minister had skimmed through for the first time in the official car on the trip to the villa.

As the politician began to speak, Höller noticed a cameraman for the state television who was filming the performance. The Minister talked about the importance of medium-sized industry for the national economy and about the fact that whether the economy of a country flourishes or collapses depends on men like Höller. Höller no longer followed the Minister's sentences; the images vanished before his eyes, partly because the strong light from the spotlights blinded him; instead he tried to locate his director's traditional costume. Then a few words without context: recession, energy problems and employment projections, ancillary wages …

Later, Höller had no idea how long the politician had spoken; applause and cheers from the faceless crowd. And suddenly his hand was again in the feeble grip of the minister, who now looked at him directly and, after a long pause, during which it became completely quiet in the park, awarded him with the title Councilor of Commerce. Renewed applause, then the cameraman and a reporter stood in front of him and the Minister, who made a few general remarks in the direction of the microphone, after which he stole himself away with a noncommittal smile into the faceless crowd. Höller refused to give the slick reporter, (as he called him), any gratuitous comments, which might even be transmitted through *oblique glances*. He said simply that getting older was no reward, and awards bored him to death; not knowing that the camera and the microphone were still recording and that this statement would be broadcast the following day between the news and the main evening programme.

In the meantime, the members of a ladies' salon orchestra had taken their seats in the pavilion. While the still-faceless crowd tackled the buffet, they played German dances, waltzes and then (especially in bad taste), when the buffet was opened, they played "Die Forelle." Because Schubert was his favorite composer, Sophie whispered in his ear, and Höller gave in. The musicians wore floor-length, white dresses and looked as if Klimt, in an unconcentrated creative frenzy, had arranged them in a lovely art nouveau composition. The faceless crowd and the Minister had to be endured, perhaps, but the ladies' salon orchestra interpretations made it even worse ...

Höller must prepare for the crucial meeting with the Mayor, and the professor does not know him. He recalls only a campaign speech on the piazza, which he had followed from the last row and, because of a defective loudspeaker, had only heard in fragments. Höller will receive no advice from him about how he should confront the man.

Höller stands deliberating in front of the open wardrobe for a long time. Then he decides on the black suit, which he had had made for the concert. The Mayor will recognize English quality and he will know immediately that his decision is of an importance which will extend far beyond this place.

Black suit, white silk shirt, dark tie, shiny black patent leather shoes, thus Höller later stands in the tower, across from his music secretary. He walks a few steps, sits down at the table and asks: Can you detect a false note?

The professor shakes his head: Not even a false semitone in your appearance!

The next morning Höller makes his way to the castle, but this time he takes a taxi instead of riding the caretaker's wife's bicycle. While he waits for the taxi in the courtyard, the cat rubs up against his legs again and, even when chasing birds or insects, will not let him out of sight.

On the journey, he deliberates over his performance, repeats sentences half aloud that he has been concocting for weeks. Finally, he tries to reassure himself: The Mayor of a place that, unlike any other, has been created for the *Fantasy*, will not oppose the project.

Next to the entrance of the castle is a *carabiniere*, who asks Höller for his subpoena, without which he could not admit him.

A crucial meeting with the Mayor, says Höller, and slips the man a twenty Euro note. Everything is at stake if I am detained!

The *carabiniere* pretends to examine Höller's identification, but actually he looks around to see if anyone has noticed, as he stashes the cash away. Finally, Höller can pass. In front of the Mayor's office, he learns from a secretary that the man is not there, because he is participating in a congress of the National Alliance in Taormina. He is expected back next week. With whom could he speak, then, regarding a cultural issue of greatest importance for the town? he asks, whereupon the young woman accompanies him to the office of the Assessor Corradi.

He is responsible for road construction, schools, kindergartens, and also for cultural affairs.

Höller knocks a few times and finally opens the door when he hears no response from inside the room. Corradi is a young man with thick, horn-rimmed glasses; measured by the thickness of the lenses, Höller supposes, the assessor must be nearly blind. It is characteristic that culture is left in the hands of such a man. Corradi is writing while Höller sits down, does not look at him, and Höller does not know whether he should speak or wait until the assessor has finished his work.

So speak, why don't you! he demands a little later, without looking up from his papers.

Höller begins with the *Fantasy*, later comes around to Castelnuovo and speaks of its ideal environment, of the *worldwide recognition* that would come to the place through the performance of the *Fantasy*. Corradi looks at him, perplexed, and Höller knows that he has been addressing a musical layman. When he calls for the demolition of the community hall, the shortsighted man snatches the telephone and whispers into the receiver. Then Gesualdo is beside Höller and seizes his upper arm, pulling him out of the room, through the corridor to the staircase. What a force lurks in the dwarf, Höller thinks, while Gesualdo pushes him down the steps.

The excitement, and the fear that Gesualdo would dislocate his arm, has aroused the adversary in his head. Dizziness, and a painful pressure in his temples when he is standing outside again. Höller sees that the *carabiniere* cannot hide his mocking smile. But that does not disturb him; he is just relieved that the dwarf has released his arm at last, and has disappeared into the castle. Again the vertigo blurs the images before his eyes. Höller knows this and remains calm, because he knows that once he sits on a bench in the castle park and swallows a pill, the usual clarity will soon return.

It is a mistake, he thinks on the bench, to negotiate with officials of the second rank. If he had spoken to the Mayor, the conversation would have taken course to his satisfaction.

BEFORE HÖLLER RETURNS to La Torre, he must achieve clarity; and not only in what he sees, but above all in his thoughts. To banish the mirage in front of his eyes is a matter of medicine. It is more difficult to forget about the unpleasant visit to the castle, because Höller does not believe that he can forget the scene in the room of the shortsighted assessor. And he should not tolerate Gesualdo's brutality, but it is for the *Fantasy*; if he were to report the deformed dwarf because of the degrading stairway scene, it could mean a delay. And Höller knows that he must not lose any time.

As he crosses the piazza, he hears the postman behind him. Signor Öller, wait! Signor Öller …

As always, the man swallows the first letter of his name, and then stands panting in front of him.

A foreign telegram, he stammers, still out of breath, although he hardly went more than ten metres. Not the English one that we expected, but still a foreign …

Höller jams a fifty Euro note into the man's hand, hoping he would return to his counter. But the clerk does not leave; he wants to see Höller's reaction to the telegram and become a confidant, to be able to tell a story to the customers in his post office. Höller is not about to appease the man's curiosity and says he will open the message later. After a hostile look, the postman takes off.

In the bar, Höller reads the message from his lawyer; the

Russian deal, and he uses Sophie's expression, has been concluded. On the conditions Höller requested. The papers were ready for his signature; he would be in the Piazza del Campo in Siena the next day around noon with the contract. And in closing, Höller might turn on his mobile phone so that they could arrange the exact meeting place.

Again, this pressure in his head. Höller searches in his jacket pocket for the painkillers, thinks he must increase the dose after the excitement he has endured at the castle. With a sip of Chianti, he takes three pills and experiences a bitter aftertaste on his palate. He drinks the glass empty, but the taste spreads. Höller eats a tuna fish sandwich. He drinks a second glass. He breathes deeply a few times. The aftertaste is gone.

The death of the Roma boy has been cleared up, he learns later from the bar's owner. It had been an accident, not murder. A set of unfortunate coincidences. The boy's parents had been delayed and did not arrive at the agreed upon time at Castelnuovo in order to fetch their son as usual and pocket his earnings. So Florentin had made his way alone on the Siena-Perugia highway. There, the driver of a light truck had seen him, too late, on a blind bend, and had run him down because he allegedly had to dodge an oncoming car and had been blinded by the low sun. The driver stopped and ran back to the boy, whom he found in a ditch. He immediately saw that he had arrived too late to help. He laid the Florentin's dead body in the bed of his truck and placed him in the spot where he had been found. In his state of shock he had meant to divert attention from himself, because the place where the body was discovered was a road that was never used. Finally, his sense of guilt had moved him to report the accident at the prefecture.

While the bar owner speculates over what will happen to

the culprit now, Höller leaves the bar and climbs into a taxi on the piazza. A lost day, he thinks on the way to La Torre. In the tower, he will take another pain pill and his heart medication, in order to clear his head for work on the *Fantasy*.

As usual, höller has chosen one of the rear tables against the wall at Café Palio. Since nine o'clock, he has been sitting on the Piazza del Campo, although he does not expect the lawyer until noon. It is the same table where he sat with Sophie a few weeks before. But that no longer means anything this morning. A few signatures on a contract that he will not read, then the factory will be sold to the Russians. His *life's work*, as Sophie had once called the business. What an absurdity, to refer to the production of parts for air conditioners as a *life's work*.

Apart from him, there is only an English couple sitting outdoors. Old people, who drink cappuccino and read a travel guide together. What peacefulness emanates from the two of them, Höller thinks. When they talk to each other, they need only a few words to agree on every issue.

Students in groups and white-collar workers cross the piazza on their way to their classrooms and offices. The first stores open half-heartedly; certainly, none of the shopkeepers are counting on a high turnover. Höller knows that tourist season is finally over; the old Englishmen are no more than a faded memory of the past summer.

After a caffè doppio, Höller drinks a Campari and soda because it helps him forget the slightly bitter taste of the tablets. After he has turned on his mobile phone, the shrill ringtone begins. The frightened couple looks around; Höller puts the phone in his jacket and waits until he is sure there that will be no more noise.

He finds text messages and a number of missed calls listed. Most are from Sophie. Höller deletes all of the entries after he has found no unknown number. Nothing that he could read is of any importance. Now he is only concerned with Brendel's *Fantasy*; everything else belongs to a past, which he sealed off months ago.

When the lawyer calls and says he is now on the highway leaving Florence and will arrive in Siena in half an hour, Höller advises him to park in the car park at Fortezza. He will be waiting for him there.

WALKING CAUSES Höller problems; due to the increased dosage the pain feels like a remote allusion, but as soon as he exerts himself even a little, because he must go uphill, the images begin to blur. The second pill he has taken for his heart condition on the way to Fortezza does not make things any clearer.

In the shadow of a huge pine tree, there is a slight improvement. Höller watches the approaching cars, but he does not know what make he should be watching for. Only one thing is clear: his lawyer will be driving a luxury model.

And sure enough, the lawyer alights from a bright red Ferrari a little later, with great effort, Höller notes, because of his corpulence and the deep seats. When, finally liberated from the prison of his sports car, he is standing next to Höller, he immediately begins to extol the advantages of the Ferrari. The fact that Höller does not react to any of his sentences does not disturb him. When they reach Santa Caterina, the lawyer finishes his description; he has neither wife nor children to support, and, after all, he cannot take it to the grave … He breaks off midsentence, and talks only of the wonderful view of the cathedral.

Over dessert in La Mangia, the lawyer, who has not offered one word about the contract yet, talks about the Ferrari again. The car is a technical marvel from a world champion factory, almost impossible to buy. There are waiting lists, and Höller cannot imagine who else has their names on these lists. Actors, presidents, CEOs, and all of them had to wait at least another year before they could pick up their cars in Maranello. But they are not here to talk about his car; the lawyer ends his praise of the red sports car, not without adding that the engine sounds like music to the ears … Then he rests his hand on the briefcase, which he has deposited on a free chair, and says that the contract, signed by the Russians, was lying in his suitcase ready. When he also signs, the deal will be clinched.

The Russians have been very cooperative, Höller learns; for them it is all about finding access to the EU economic market through acquisitions. He had rarely negotiated transactions of this size with such a responsive partner. They had even accepted Höller's single condition without hesitation: Unterloibnegger will continue to lead the enterprise under the Russian owners. When, after the successful conclusion of negotiations, he had asked the Russians what desires he might satisfy for them, they had not reacted, to his surprise, like most of those that he had done business with in the past. Instead of the usual introduction to women or casino invitations, the Russians wanted traditional costumes like the one the operations director was wearing.

Höller and his lawyer drink coffee later in the Palio. After the contract is signed, the lawyer hands Höller a few newspapers. They contained articles about Sophie and the minister's trial, in which she fought, to the surprise of all of the experts and others who observed the trial, for an acquittal. An acquittal based on lack of evidence always leaves a bad taste, because most people consider the acquitted person guilty in such cases. Everyone in the media had speculated for months just how high the fine would be and whether or not the court would send the minister to jail, but in her closing argument Sophie had attacked the public prosecutor. And with a rhetorical brilliance they would talk about for years.

I will read the articles when I return to La Torre, Höller says, thinking only about how he could get rid of his lawyer as quickly as possible. But that was child's play, because the lawyer was already thinking about his Ferrari again. After the successful conclusion of two transactions, (in addition to selling Höller's business he had acquired a Czech steel mill for a Luxembourg consortium), he was going to treat himself to a few weeks' holiday. He will drive the Ferrari through all the regions of Italy; after all, an Italian car should only be broken-in in Italy.

Fortunately it is an Italian car, Höller said when they parted beside the Ferrari. With a Japanese car, the matter would be more complicated. Then, with a hellish roar from the chrome exhaust pipes that the lawyer would call music, the car soon disappeared behind a bend.

As HÖLLER EXITS the taxi in front of La Torre, the professor comes running towards him. He swings the rolled up *Corriere* above his head like a sword. The *buffone* has finally gone crazy, he shouts, and then stands, out of breath, in front of Höller, who cannot understand the excitement. The professor is still swinging the newspaper at invisible adversaries. When he is breathing evenly again, he opens the *Corriere* and reads: *The Prime Minister wants a more modest art. Tiepolo's painting*

"Truth Unveiled by Time" has been reworked, so the bare breasts are no longer visible. *In that hall where the government holds press conferences, they do not want anything that will offend television viewers.* And the clueless constituency had elected this madman for the third time.

Do not waste your time with side issues, Höller tries to calm the man down; concentrate on your tasks, think of the *Fantasy*; the training of the ushers.

The professor rolls up the *Corriere* again and whispers, it was true, what makes people like the megalomaniac ladies from Milan so dangerous: the ignorance of people. Then, offended, he goes into the house.

After a shower, Höller sits in the tower room with the newspapers that his lawyer has given him. He knows that the professor will not trouble him that evening. He will pout and think about the decline of the country; he will eventually end up on his divorce proceedings; the baseness of women and the corruption of the judiciary; corruption and libido will form an impenetrable mix from which he will, completely distraught and exhausted, fall sleep.

He must draft a plan that will convince the Mayor. The man must not be allowed to doubt him for a second. The performance with the short-sighted assessor cannot be repeated. A short conversation, then the Mayor must grant permission for the demolition of the town hall. Without the least objection. He will envision the sudden fame of Castelnuovo after the concert. Of the masses who will visit the place where Brendel has played the *Fantasy*. The *Russian deal* gives him some latitude. The only thing lacking is the Mayor's consent. And he is still waiting for the English letter.

AGAIN THIS dizziness that blurs all of the contours. The distance between the attacks is growing shorter. Höller feels his way along the wall to the west window, which he opens. Despite the damp cold, which moves into the tower. Soon he is breathing easier. He thinks about swallowing another pill for his heart. Then he thinks about the doctors' warnings and sits down at the desk with the newspapers.

He sees pictures of Sophie; reads articles about the trial against the Minister, of whose guilt all the papers are convinced. In one picture, he is seen next to Sophie. Pale and stooping, he stands beside her. Looking into the void, while Sophie enjoys her victory. There is more to read about in most of the articles than the doubtful judgement. The Minister has been cleared; after a few days he will vanish into thin air. A marginal figure, because Sophie occupies the centre. Entire sections from her closing argument are quoted. Höller reads the sentences like the sentences about a stranger; he sees the pictures as if they were pictures of someone unknown, and skims ahead. He scans headlines that do not interest him until he jumps up in horror.

Pianist Alfred Brendel: I Deliberately Choose to Stop Playing These Pieces

The Austrian pianist of the century, Alfred Brendel, has, for the first time given reasons for the upcoming end of his concert career.

"I always had the feeling that I play these pieces of my own free will. And now I am deliberately choosing to stop," says Brendel.

The 77-year-old adds: "There are no physical reasons."

He admits, though, that he can no longer play pieces as physically exhausting as Schubert's "Wanderer Fantasy" …

"In the last few years I have carefully selected what I play and have set the athletic pieces aside," Brendel says. Brendel, who will appear on the stage for the last time on the 18th of December in Vienna, will thereafter only make public appearances for lectures, readings and discussions …

Höller reads the article again and again; after the last word, he immediately begins again with the title. He thinks: a newspaper hoax. One of his father's phrases suddenly comes to mind. You can write anything on paper, and nowhere are there as many lies as in newspapers. But not in a paper like this, Höller knows, and reads faster and faster until he is whispering the text without looking at the paper.

The walls of the tower are in flames. Gray-orange tongues of fire dance to the rhythm of the *Fantasy*. A crackling and hissing in the walls, which are pushing now from all sides toward the centre.

The burning walls will crush him if he does not get outside immediately … Höller thinks and stumbles down the steep stairs. He pushes open the heavy wooden door and stands in the yard. He sees the tri-colored cat on the run from the flames, disappearing behind the farm buildings.

As bright as day now is the night, from which he must save the *Fantasy*.

Höller is running down the hill from La Torre. He forgets the burning in his lungs, his racing pulse, the dancing images. Cypress trees and vines tear themselves up from their roots and jump from the loose earthwork.

Then there are voices on the square in front of the caretaker's house. Innumerable voices, but because of the sudden darkness there are no faces that belong to those voices.

He admits, though, that he can no longer play pieces as physically exhausting as Schubert's "Wanderer Fantasy" …

Maybe these voices will save the *Fantasy*?

I always had the feeling that I play these pieces of my own free will. And now I am deliberately choosing to stop …

Höller stands where the road opens into the square in front of the caretaker's house. The voices are getting closer. And then he sees the first face. The Roma boy is running towards him.

What a surprise, Signor Brendel! he shouts. Again and again: what a surprise! The disaster, the interrogation in the room of the caretaker's house, all lies, thinks Höller and recognises the caretaker and the lawyer Panella a few metres behind Florentin. The professor follows them with the ushers in their black uniforms. After a brief look, Höller is reassured. None of them is limping; Giuseppe's Libyan leg cannot be seen.

The light glistens ever more brightly; he holds a protective hand over his eyes. Through a gap between his fingers, he sees the road workers' truck. On the truck bed stands the piano from the Bösendorfer concert hall. And then the images fade into white and an eerie silence falls over the square, like the faraway opening chords of the *Fantasy*.

Note
Quotations (modified) by Alfred Brendel, Günter Brus, Ermanno Cavazzoni, Luigi Malerba, Cees Nooteboom and from the magazine *Panorama* (No. 1266, Milan 1990).

About the Author

Günther Freitag was born in 1952 in Feldkirch/Vorarlberg. He studied history and German language and literature in Graz, and also enrolled for piano at the Conservatory. He wrote plays and prose works. In 1985, he took part in the Bachmann Competition. The author has received several awards including the Forum Stadtpark Literature Prize of the city of Graz (1982); a grant from the Province of Styria (1990); and the Culture Prize of the city of Leoben (1992). He lives in Leoben/Styria.

About the Translator

Eugene H. Hayworth is an Associate Professor for the University Libraries at the University of Colorado Boulder. His first book, *Fever Vision: the Life and Works of Coleman Dowell*, was published by Dalkey Archive Press in 2007. He became interested in the work of Günther Freitag while living in Berlin as the recipient of a Fulbright Scholarship to teach at Humboldt University.